What they say abou

'I wish I men ... age 6

'I love how it takes you into a new world.' *Alice, age 10*

'Sophi ... r and
turns ... ories.'
Camero

'The s ... *Elliott,*
age 9¼

'Sophi ... rised.'
Ashleig

'The illustrations are amazing.' *Sarah, age 12*

'. . . six rumbustious adventures, it enjoys Blytonesque jollities and gorgeous grotesques drawn by Ted Dewan.' *Amanda Craig, The Times*

THOMAS TREW
AND THE FLYING HUNTSMAN
THE

SOPHIE MASSON

Illustrated by Ted Dewan

*Hodder
Children's
Books*

A division of Hachette Children's Books

For Colm and Finnbar and Marcella

Dear Reader,

Do you wish you could leave the ordinary world and go into an extraordinary one, full of fun and magic and adventure – and danger? You do? Well, so does Thomas Trew – and one grey London afternoon, his wish comes true!

Two amazing people come calling – a dwarf called Adverse Camber and a bright little lady named Angelica Eyebright. They tell Thomas he's a Rymer and that he has a destiny in their world, the world of the Hidden People. And they ask him to come and live in their village, Owlchurch, deep in the Hidden World.

It's a world of magic – what the Hidden People call 'pishogue'. It's a world of extraordinary places and people – the Ariels, who live in the sky; the Seafolk, who live in the ocean; the Montaynards, who live in the rocks and mountains; the Uncouthers, who live deep underground, and the Middlers, who live on the surface of the earth. Not everyone in the Hidden World is pleasant or friendly, and some of them, like the Uncouthers, are very nasty indeed . . .

All kinds of adventures are waiting for Thomas in the Hidden World. And this is just one of them. Look out for the others!

ONE

Thomas took a deep breath and leaned forward, very carefully. He was standing on tiptoes on a rather wobbly chair. And he was standing on that chair because he was about to blow out the ten candles on his birthday cake.

This was no ordinary cake. It was enormous, and shaped like a palace. The domed palace roof was of blue and gold icing, the pillars were made of pure white spun sugar, and it had sparkling, clear toffee windows. Thomas thought the whole thing looked less like a cake and more like the kind of precious object you put behind glass. He didn't say that out loud, though, because he didn't want to hurt

Cumulus Zephyrus's feelings. The Owlchurch baker had worked on his creation for days and was very proud of it.

Thomas blew hard. The silver candles flickered, flared, then went out. Cumulus clicked his fingers. At once, six little toy soldiers in white and gold uniforms, holding tiny silver trumpets, popped out of the palace's front door. In unison, they lifted their trumpets and began to play 'Happy Birthday'. Everyone

2

in the Apple Tree Café joined in, Thomas's friends Pinch and Patch loudest of all.

There were lots of people crowded into the cosy main room of the café. Practically all of Owlchurch was there, from the Mayor Angelica Eyebright to the Trickster Hinkypunk Hobthrust, from the dwarf Adverse Camber to the bookseller Monotype Eberhardt. There were even some people from the rival village of Aspire, including the glamorous Mayors, the Lady Pandora and Mr Tamblin. Thomas was popular in both places, and his tenth birthday was a big event.

The soldiers played 'For He's a Jolly Good Fellow', and then bowed to Thomas. Cumulus clicked his fingers. As suddenly as they'd appeared, the soldiers vanished once again.

'Well, Thomas,' beamed Cumulus, 'what do you think of my cake?'

'It's amazing! I've never seen anything like it before.'

'It's a model of Duke Nimbus's palace in

Seraphimia, the city of the Ariels,' said Cumulus, happily. The big baker was an Ariel himself, though he now lived in Middler lands.

Thomas said, carefully, 'It seems a pity to cut it.'

Pinch glared at him. 'Don't be so silly. It's made to be eaten, not kept like some old fossil!'

'And it won't be, I'm sure,' said Cumulus, smiling. He handed Thomas the big cake knife. 'Try it. You'll get a surprise.'

Everyone watched as Thomas cut into the side of the cake. Immediately, a perfect slice tumbled out of the cake – but the wall was left quite whole!

Cumulus explained, 'Just a bit of pishogue I use for very special occasions. You can cut and cut lots of fine fat slices, but the cake will still look perfect. It's a cut-and-come-again cake. The magic will last for days.'

'Oh, wow,' breathed Thomas. Eagerly, he attacked the palace wall again, and cut slice after perfect slice. But the cake stayed whole.

What's more, it tasted wonderful!

When everyone had eaten their fill, Angelica Eyebright jumped up on a chair, and called for silence.

'Thomas, this is a very special day, and we want to make it even more special. Now, you've been with us for quite a while now, and you've seen quite a lot of the Hidden World. But there's one country you don't know yet. And that's Ariel country. How would you like a day trip today to Seraphimia, the capital city of the Ariels? With Pinch and Patch,' she went on.

'And me as a guide,' said Cumulus Zephyrus, proudly.

'Well, what do you say?' said Angelica.

'Oh, yes, *please!*' Thomas cried.

'Yes! Wow! Excellent!' shrieked the twins, hopping up and down.

'I've modified Metallicus specially for the trip,' beamed Adverse Camber. Metallicus was Adverse's pride and joy, his cranky talking car.

Mr Tamblin and Lady Pandora raised their eyebrows. Mr Tamblin said, languidly, 'That old rattle-trap? Don't you need something a little more elegant, to arrive in Ariel country? What about our car?'

Adverse glared at him. 'Nobody asked you to—' he began, but Angelica cut him off.

'Thanks for the offer, Tamblin, but we're going in Metallicus. Now then, children, we just need to give you a dose of airflower juice. That will help you to breathe normally up there. Then we'll be off. It's not that far, if we go by Cumulus's short cut. But we want to pack in as much as we can in one day. It's not a good idea to be out on sky-roads after dark.'

'Why not?' said Thomas's father Gareth, sharply.

Angelica shrugged. 'They're not that well looked after, they've got a few potholes, that's all,' she said, lightly. 'But don't worry, Gareth. We'll take care of our birthday boy. Of course, you could come with us if you like,' she added.

'No thanks. I'm not very fond of flying at the best of times,' said Gareth, with a little shudder. 'And in Metallicus . . . no, not really. Well, if you're quite sure it will be OK . . .'

'Cumulus is coming with us as our guide,' said Angelica. 'And Captain Mercury, the Ariels' messenger, would have told us if there were any problems. We'd never put Thomas into danger.'

Thomas hardly heard what they were saying. He'd caught a tiny, amazing glimpse of Ariel country, when they'd had to fly over the sea in one of his other adventures. But this time, he would actually visit it properly! How exciting!

He didn't know yet quite *how* exciting it would turn out to be . . .

TWO

'Oh, oh, oh,' groaned Metallicus in his grating voice, as Adverse engaged the gears. 'I've changed my mind about this flying lark. Don't want to do it any more. I'm not some kind of dodgy magic carpet, you know!'

'Metallicus! Just get going, or we'll lose Cumulus,' said Adverse, crossly. 'And stop your whining. Or I'll have to make another change and turn off your voice-box.'

'You wouldn't dare,' grated the car sharply, but now it started forward, jerkily, crossly. It kangaroo-hopped along the road, then smoothed out, gathering speed.

'Hold on!' shouted Adverse, as the car rattled

and shook, and the engine roared. Just above them, his wings spread wide, Cumulus hovered anxiously, waiting for them to take off. Thomas and the twins braced themselves and clutched at the back seat, excitedly and a little nervously.

'Oh, oh, oh, here I go!' groaned Metallicus, very loudly, and with a wrenching, grinding sound, and a rattle that threatened to shake Thomas's teeth from his head, the car rose heavily and reluctantly into the air. Almost immediately, it bumped down a little way, and everyone yelled. But in an instant, it had righted itself again, and rose up, up, up, jerkily at first, then more and more smoothly. Very soon, it was riding along the air currents and cloud-paths as easily as it usually ran along the roads on earth.

Adverse took out a handkerchief from his pocket and wiped his face. 'Thank goodness we're up,' he said. 'For a moment, there, I thought that—'

'You did well,' interrupted Angelica. 'You and Metallicus.'

'Glad to hear someone's not forgotten about me,' said the car, tetchily. 'After all, it was me took the biggest risk, and—'

'Yes, yes, yes,' said Adverse, impatiently. 'You can praise yourself later. Right now, keep sight of Cumulus. Look, he's just turned that corner . . .'

'Do you take me for an idiot?' huffed the car. 'Unlike some, I know just what's what, you know!'

Thomas and the twins stared out of the windows, at the cloud-scape unfolding all around them. Soon, they left the open sky behind and climbed up into an enclosed white cloud-valley between a range of rather sinister thundercloud-coloured peaks. There was no open sky to be seen here. There was a narrow road winding like a stream in the valley, but no sign of any dwellings. It was very quiet, and very still, lit with a strange blue-tinged light as the sun struck weakly through the peaks. This created odd shadows in the valley, of almost but not quite human and animal shape, which drifted like a kind of shadow-puppet play over the unearthly scene.

Angelica turned around. She said, 'This is the shadow-land. It's by far the quickest route to the heart of Ariel country, but we wouldn't go this way if Cumulus wasn't with us.'

'What is it, exactly?' breathed Thomas.

'It's an in-between place,' said Angelica. 'A half-place. No one lives there. And it shifts and changes with the passing of the days. It never looks the same. Ariels know it better than anybody, and they made this road. But they would not live here.'

'Why not?' said Pinch.

Angelica pointed at the shadows. 'These are things left unfinished from the beginning of the world. There was something wrong about them, some flaw. And so they have never become real, if you see what I mean. They have no purpose. No voice. They only exist here, as shadows of what might have been.'

Thomas stared out at the drifting shapes that filled the valley. He said, 'This is a sad place.'

'Yes, Thomas, it is,' said Angelica, quietly. 'That's why no one wants to live here.'

I wish we could be out of here, Thomas thought, with a shiver. There was something frightening about that quiet, still place, with its drifting, aimless shadows.

Very soon, he got his wish. Reaching the head of the valley, they suddenly emerged into sunlit air and the edge of a blue sky shimmering like a calm ocean. Dotted amongst the blue were islands of fluffy cloud, each with a narrow silver tower, like a lighthouse.

Angelica said, 'Those are the Ariel lookouts. We're very close now. You see, that short cut through the shadow-land saved us a good deal of time. It was worth doing.'

Thomas looked quickly behind him. There was no trace of the shadow-land. It had completely disappeared.

Adverse pressed a lever near the steering wheel. Metallicus slid on to the blue sky-ocean, and then settled gently on it, moving rather like a hovercraft. The air was of a glorious brightness and clarity, the sun shining directly above them.

They made good headway. Following Cumulus, who dipped and soared in front of them, they hovered gently between the cloud-islands, passing the silver towers. Close to, they were very strange, shimmering, more like reflections in a mirror than solid objects. And they had no windows or doors.

'How does anyone get in there?' said Thomas. 'I mean, to keep a lookout.'

'Oh, nobody's actually *in* them. They're long-distance lookouts,' said Angelica. 'There's a control room for them in Duke Nimbus's palace. The Ariels can see everything out here from there.'

Just as they passed the second-last tower, light flashed from it, and bathed the car, for an instant, in blinding brightness. Then it flashed off again.

'They've spotted us, now,' said Adverse Camber. 'We're expected – but if we weren't, very soon we'd be seeing a squadron of Ariel soldiers coming to meet us.'

'But who are their enemies?' said Thomas. 'Surely the Uncouthers can't get all the way up here . . .' The Uncouthers, who lived underground, were the enemies of most of the rest of the Hidden World. Thomas had come up against them more than once.

'No, the Uncouthers can't,' agreed Angelica. 'But they can send agents – that's happened before. Besides, there's outlaws, pirates, and thieves, working on their own account. The sky-country is a bit like the sea-country. It's huge and not all parts of it are settled. All kinds of strange and dangerous people live in its remote and far-flung places.'

Soon they swept past the last cloud-island, and

sailed into a narrow strait that led to two big white headlands like a pair of gigantic gates. Past the headlands, and now they were in an enormous lagoon of a deep turquoise blue. In the middle of this sky-lagoon rose the towers and domes of a shining island city. For the first time, there were people about – Ariels, that is. To Thomas's surprise, they were of all sizes, not just huge like Cumulus. Though all were winged, some were as tiny and dainty as butterflies or dragonflies, whilst others were the size of birds, from small to large, and still others were gigantic like Cumulus. Some had ragged white wings, others wings of shimmering translucent colours, still others narrow, knife-shaped silver wings. Some rode the air currents on their wings, others skimmed the surface of the sky-lagoon like something out of a ballet, others still lounged on piles of cushions in double-prowed open vessels like great gondolas, or piloted airships shaped like golden bubbles that Adverse said were called 'sun-sailors'.

'Oh, look, there are some children!' said Patch, nudging Thomas. An Ariel family was gliding past – two elegant parents with golden skin and silver hair and wings that rippled like living metal, and two smaller versions, with bright little faces and miniature wings. The Ariel parents ignored Metallicus and its passengers but the Ariel children turned their heads and stared at Thomas and the twins, their eyes almost popping out of their heads. Pinch made a rude face at them. Their mouths fell open. Jostling each other, they flew quickly after their parents.

'Pinch, you are awful,' hissed Patch, speaking low so Angelica and Adverse wouldn't hear. 'You scared them.'

'That'll teach them to stare,' retorted Pinch.

'Not like *you're* staring,' snapped Patch.

'That's different. I'm staring 'cos it's amazing. But they were staring like we were monsters or something.'

'They've probably never seen Middlers or

humans before,' said Thomas, rather absently, staring at the city below him. 'They don't know what we are.'

It looked somehow familiar, he thought. Yes! He knew what it reminded him of. His dad had a picture of Venice hanging up in his study back in London, and that was what Seraphimia looked like, beautiful Venice floating on its lagoon. Just as in Venice, there were canals everywhere, only these were of milky white cloud and blue sky. The gondolas and sun-sailors zipped in and out of them. A vast palace white as spun sugar, with a dome of sun-gilt and sky-blue, dominated the skyline.

'Wow! It's just like your cake — only much, much bigger!' said Patch, impressed.

'Wouldn't it be nice if it was really a cake?' said Pinch, licking his lips.

In front of the palace was a huge square. Enormous statues stood in the square — a winged horse, a winged lion, a griffin, and several Ariels. Beyond the palace square the

city sprawled: grand houses fronting canals, narrow little alleys full of bright shops, hump-backed bridges leading to beautiful little gardens full of sky-flowers and tinkling fountains. It was quite the most enchanting place Thomas had ever seen.

Without warning, Metallicus began its descent. Thomas's stomach lurched. Adverse shouted, 'Steady on, steady on, old boy, you'll make everyone sick!'

The car shuddered, straightened out and came rather more smoothly down, down, down, landing at last with a rather grinding halt at the quay by the edge of the harbour. 'Best I could do,' grumbled the car, 'I'm going to need a good rest now, after what you've put me through.'

Before Adverse could answer, Cumulus appeared. He opened the back door, and they came out.

'Welcome to Seraphimia, children,' he said, beaming. 'Now, flying does give one an appetite, doesn't it?' He turned to Angelica. 'There's a superb bakery only a few steps from here. They make the best moon-cakes ever. Can I take the children for a bite there while you register us at the visitors' centre?'

'Sure,' smiled Angelica. 'But don't be too long.'

'Back in a jiff.' As the children hurried along in Cumulus's gliding wake, across the quay, the big baker said, 'It's one of my few regrets, about living in Middler country. The moon-cakes just don't turn out the way they do here. That's why I've given up making them . . .'

They turned into a narrow alley, running down one side of a canal. The alley was lined with cosy little shops, with bow-fronted windows that gave on to the street. 'The bakers' quarter,' said Cumulus. 'All the shops here are bakeries, pastry-cooks' shops, that sort of thing. Come on.'

But the children couldn't hurry. There was too much to look at! Behind the bow-fronted windows were fantastic displays: cakes big enough to feed a whole village, and tiny cakes that would hardly satisfy an ant. There were cakes shaped like buildings and animals and gondolas and sun-sailors. There were cakes with multicoloured icing and silver sprinkles and pink sugar roses, and cakes with a plain golden-brown top that even from outside smelled like heaven. And there was bread, too: crusty twists and rolls and plaits and loaves, piled high in great baskets. There were savoury things, as well: hot pies and pasties and rolls and puddings, bursting with rich and tasty fillings.

Thomas's mouth watered. The twins' tongues were hanging out. But Cumulus beckoned them on to the end of the row of shops. 'This is the place,' he said, pointing up at the sign which read, 'Signora Anafiela's Bakery'.

It smelled great. And looked wonderful. Gleaming display-cases full of cakes and pies and bread lined one side of the cosy shop, a counter was at the other side, and there were some tables and chairs set out in the middle. A few customers sat at them, eating and drinking. They turned to look at the newcomers curiously as they walked up to the counter.

The baker was a small Ariel, not much taller than Angelica. She had golden-brown skin the exact colour of a cake top and smiley eyes the colour of raisins. From her shoulders sprouted wings of a soft dark brown, decorated with black spots like eyes, rather like the wings of a moth.

'May I help you?' she said, her eyes bright and curious. She waved a hand at a tray of little iced cakes. 'A wish-cake, perhaps? It's a new line of mine.'

'They look lovely,' said Cumulus, smiling, 'but actually, we'd like four moon-cakes. Four moon-cakes, for myself and my friends. Three of us are from the Hidden World; the fourth' – here he reached over and touched Thomas on the head – 'is a human. But not an ordinary human. A Rymer.'

'Well, well! A Rymer!' said the baker, and coming around the side of the counter, she shook hands with them all. The customers watched curiously. Thomas felt embarassed.

'We haven't had a Rymer here in years!' went on the baker. 'Or Middlers, indeed,' she added, glancing at Pinch and Patch.

'We're here on a flying visit,' said Cumulus, grandly. 'We have an appointment with Duke Nimbus in a short while, and then a tour of the city. But I thought the first stop should be here, to the best moon-cake baker in the whole country.'

'Well, how very nice of you, sir! You must let me have the honour of giving you these moon-cakes free,' she said, and reaching inside a display-case, she pulled out – rather to Thomas's disappointment – four of the plainest-looking cakes in the shop. They weren't particularly big, either, though not as small as the wish-cakes – rather like a patty-cake, only a little larger. 'These were baked this morning,' she went on. 'They're very fresh.'

'Thank you so much,' said Cumulus, eagerly. 'It's such a treat, Signora Anafiela, to see a real moon-cake again.'

'How long have you been away, sir?' she asked.

'Well, I went off to live in Middler country a hundred years or so ago,' said Cumulus, 'and now I have a bakery in Owlchurch and I . . .'

He was off, chatting away to the baker, while behind his back Pinch made a despairing face. 'I wish he'd stop talking! And I wish we could get more than one little cake! I'm going to starve!' he muttered.

'Maybe it'll be a cut-and-come-again thing, like my birthday cake,' Thomas said, hopefully.

'I wish we'd brought some of that along with us!' said Patch, wistfully.

'If only he hadn't made such a huge one!' groaned Pinch.

'If only who hadn't made such a big what?' said Cumulus, suddenly turning back to them.

Pinch went red. 'Nothing,' he muttered.

'Very well, then, let's go. And thank you for your kindness, Signora Anafiela. We will greatly enjoy the cakes.'

'I hope so. It was a pleasure to meet you all. I hope you'll enjoy your visit,' said the baker, smiling, and went to open the door for them. 'Oh, one more thing,' she added. 'You had no problem on the road?'

'No,' said Cumulus, sharply. 'Why should we?'

'Then there was no sign of Euryon? There's a rumour that he's on the move, and is headed this way. It could be just a rumour, of course.'

'There was no sign of him anywhere we went,' said Cumulus, uncomfortably.

The baker shot him a bright glance. 'Well, make sure you're not on the roads at dark. Just in case.'

THREE

Back in the street, Cumulus said, fretfully, 'Oh dear! When Angelica hears of Euryon being on the rampage again, she'll want to go home straight away.'

The children looked at each other. 'Who's Euryon?' said Thomas.

'The flying huntsman. A notorious outlaw, from the wildest region of the sky.'

'An outlaw?' said Pinch. 'Like our father?'

'Oh no,' said Cumulus. 'Your father's a good sort. This one isn't.'

'But what does he *do*?' said Thomas.

'He's a storm-giant and goes charging about on his big brute of a winged horse, black as night, with his ravening pack of red-eyed dogs. Most of the time he stays in his own country, hunting and riding about and making things miserable for any travellers foolish enough to go near. But sometimes he gets it into his head to go hunting further afield. He can't come into Seraphimia – there's very strong magic keeping him out of there – but he raids outlying castles and villas and cottages. He steals whatever he can get his hands on, and destroys houses. But the worse thing is, sometimes he hunts people.'

'People?' breathed Thomas.

'Yes. If they're lucky, he'll only kidnap them and hold them to ransom. If not – well – they never see their home again. He likes to play cruel games with his victims . . .'

'Why don't the Ariels stop him?' cried Thomas.

'They can't,' sighed Cumulus. 'Storm-giants are from the beginning of time, from the morning of the world. He's not an Ariel, and his power is stronger than theirs, when he's on the rampage. They have no real hold over him. All they can do is keep him out of the city, and try and repair the damage he's done afterwards.'

'Can he . . . can he do anything to us?' faltered Patch.

'Not while we're here,' said Cumulus, grimly. 'Trouble is that once you're out on the open road, you're fair game, if he happens to be around.' He sighed deeply. 'It's such a pity. We'll have to leave for home straight away. Ah well! It can't be helped. At least we've been warned. And he always hunts at night, never during the day, so we should be safe enough.' He smiled at their anxious faces. 'Don't worry, it'll be OK. Let's forget about him and concentrate on more important matters – such as eating our moon-cakes!'

And they *were* delicious, light and sweet, with a hint of lemon. Though they were small, and so light, they were really satisfying, the flavours lingering on and on. It was the most amazing feeling, like eating one delicious cake after another and not feeling sick at all!

Cumulus looked a little happier now. 'They're just as good as I remember them,' he declared.

'Mmm,' said Pinch, licking his lips, 'I reckon I could do with another one or two or three of these!'

'We'll buy some more before we go back home,' said Cumulus.

'Oh, yes, please!' said Patch. 'What's in the moon-cakes?' she asked, and Cumulus began explaining.

But Thomas didn't listen much. He trailed a little behind the others, looking into all the shop windows. He wondered how long it took, to get as good as this. Did they spend years and years on it, centuries maybe?

Suddenly, he heard a little whine, close behind him. He turned around. There stood a tiny brown dog, wagging its tail. It had bright dark eyes and funny little spiky wings. It looked at Thomas and gave a soft bark. Thomas said, 'What's up, little dog?'

The little creature whined again. Its bright eyes looked up, pleadingly. 'What's wrong?' said Thomas, and he bent down to touch it.

At once, his tongue went numb, then his face, and then his whole head. He felt a sharp tingling in his hands and his feet. He felt himself flung with great force against the stone wall of the alley. He tried to shout; but his tongue was like a block of wood in his mouth. He tried to move; but his limbs would not obey him. In fact, he couldn't even move his eyes. They were like bits of unmoving glass, and his body felt as though it had been turned to stone. Only his thoughts kept whirling round and round in panicky circles, like flies trapped in a jar. What had happened to him? Why hadn't the others noticed? What was he going to do?

* * *

It wasn't until the others had reached the end of the alley that they turned around to look for Thomas. But he was nowhere to be seen.

'He must have gone into a shop,' said Pinch, and he and Patch ran back the way they'd come, looking into every shop. But he wasn't there. By this time, Cumulus was alerted, too, and together they looked everywhere they could think of, behind rubbish bins, and down side alleys, but in vain. He was not there. He was not anywhere. He had simply vanished into thin air.

'Where is he? What's happened?' wailed Patch.

'I bet you the flying huntsman's got him,' said Pinch. 'I bet you he's going to hold him to ransom!'

'Shut up, Pinch,' snapped Cumulus. He was very pale. 'That's a ridiculous idea. There is no way Euryon can come into the city, I told you.'

'Maybe he's thought of a way . . .' began Pinch, but stopped when he saw Cumulus's expression. 'OK, then what happened?'

'How should I know?' said the Ariel, grimly. 'There's only one thing we can do. And that's to tell Angelica and Adverse and the Duke at once.'

'He can't have been taken very far!' said Pinch. 'I bet he's still here somewhere . . .'

Yes, I am, I am, thought poor Thomas, desperately. He could hear and see everything that was going on, but he couldn't move a muscle or make a sound. He was held flat against the wall as if his limbs had suction caps, but though the twins and Cumulus had run by him more than once, *they hadn't seen him*. I've been thinned, he thought, suddenly. I've been made invisible. But it's not the usual kind of thinning, that you do yourself. There, you could move about and speak and do everything as normal, except people wouldn't see you. This time, it was as if he was paralysed. He tried to think his way out of thinning, but it was like struggling against bands of steel. He couldn't even remember the words for it. He couldn't do anything at all, except watch as his friends ran past him again, calling his name. Then they ran out of the alley, on their way to raise the alarm, and he was alone.

The wall was very cold against his back. Usually, when you were thinned, you'd feel itchy – an itch that would start off mildly, but then get worse and worse as the thinning wore on. It was one of the reasons why humans couldn't stay thinned for long. But this time, he felt no itch. And his limbs had stopped tingling. Everything was heavy, numb, cold.

And then something – someone – he couldn't see who or what, his eyes could not move at all – picked him up, as if he'd been a shop dummy, and flung him over their shoulder. He hung down helplessly, stiff as a board, while the person trudged away with him. Thomas tried to see who was holding him, but his unmoving eyes could see only cobblestones. He could hear noises; crowd noises, bustling, cheerful sounds. Were they in the square? Surely someone would see him? The Ariels had strong magic, Cumulus had said so. Surely then they'd be able to see through this spell?

But nothing happened to free him. Now the cheerful crowd noise was being left behind, and his captor turned another corner. He walked unhurriedly down a street, paused halfway down it, took something from his pocket. A key. He was unlocking a door. Thomas heard it open, and then shut. He heard a bolt being set across. A thin, precise man's voice said, 'Not long now, lad,' and then he felt himself being carried up a long, long flight of stairs, swinging helplessly like a bag of dirty washing.

At last, the man stopped. Thomas felt himself being flung down and tried to put out his hands to save himself. But they would not obey him. But at least he did not hurt himself when he fell on to the hard floor. He was still numb.

A finger touched the corners of his eyes, lightly. The voice said a soft word. At once, Thomas's eyes started to move. He could swivel them about in their sockets once more. And he could see his own body, though he still could not move it at all. But at least he could see where he was.

FOUR

He was lying on a thick rug, on the floor of a big, round room, high up by the look of it, and filled with light. The walls were yellow, and there was a big window set into one wall, and a skylight in the domed ceiling up above. A large telescope was set up near the window, and near it was a table, piled with papers and books and instruments. Close by the table was a golden cage on a stand. The cage was empty.

Thomas heard the swish of robes behind him, then the voice, saying, 'Let's be having a proper look at you, then,' and the man came to stand over Thomas. He didn't look like the kind of person who would spellbind and kidnap a complete stranger. He didn't look strong or wicked enough. He was a tall, thin Ariel, with ragged grey wings emerging from thin shoulders under his plain dark robe and cloak, and a vague, friendly face with mild blue eyes peering behind big spectacles.

'Hmm,' said the Ariel. 'You're a bit thin and small, aren't you? Still, you'll have to do. Now, then – first things first.'

He went to the table and picked something up. Horrified, Thomas saw it was a knife – a wickedly sharp, thin knife. Desperately, Thomas tried to force his body to move. But he couldn't even scream. The Ariel was going to kill him and there was nothing he could do! He could only watch in sheer terror as the Ariel came closer and closer, as he knelt down beside Thomas, raised the knife high, brought it down and . . . slashed at the air near Thomas's feet! *Swish, swish*, went the knife, harmlessly, slashing at the air, again and again. Stunned, Thomas stared blankly. What was going on? Was the Ariel playing some kind of horrible game with him, like a cat playing with a mouse?

Then suddenly, the man gave a cry of triumph. Dropping the knife with a clatter, he darted forward.

'Come on, come on, my beauty,' he crooned. Was there something – something shapeless, formless, clinging to his hands like a sort of dust . . . a mist . . . a fog? The man tugged, at thin air, it seemed. He stood up, and kept tugging, grunting with the effort. And suddenly, there was a kind of popping sound, and something flickered into view in his hands.

Something thin and small and wispy, of a misty grey colour that gradually darkened till it was quite black. Thomas stared. The thing looked like a column of smoke, like a bit of dirty steam. He had no idea what it actually was.

The Ariel took a deep breath and blew on the thing. White light shot out from his mouth, enveloping the misty thing in a kind of transparent globe. The thing trembled, shook, wavered, and then began to change shape, to blow up . . . up . . . up like a balloon. It stayed black, but now it began to assume a form – or rather the outline of a form – the outline of a boy . . . Look, there was the head, the nose, the hands, the arms, the legs, the feet, the outline of clothes, the . . .

In a flash, Thomas understood. It was a shadow! His own shadow! The Ariel had cut his shadow away from him! He had stolen it from him! But why? Why? What could he possibly want with it?

The shadow flickered darkly in the globe of

light. The Ariel turned from it, back towards Thomas. 'Can't leave you like this, my boy. Someone might find you.' He bent down to Thomas, who tried to plead with his eyes. Please, please let me go. Please, please don't hurt me. Please, please leave me alone!

The Ariel took no notice. He touched Thomas's forehead, lightly. He muttered something – and suddenly, Thomas felt feeling returning to his body, a jolting, electrifying ripple of feeling that travelled all the way down to his toes and flew into his hands. For the flash of an instant, he could move – and he used that time to jump to his feet and fling himself at the Ariel, making him fall over backwards with a shout of surprise. Staggering, his legs shaking, Thomas tried to make a run for the door – but the Ariel had recovered, and shouted something very loudly. Instantly, Thomas felt himself picked up bodily and hurled through the air. Shooting pains zipped up his legs, his arms; he felt his body folding in on itself, shrinking, shrinking . . . Then all at once the door of the golden cage flew open, and he was flung inside. The door slammed shut, and he was trapped!

He threw himself against the bars, to no avail. He could still move, but it was hopeless, he was caught fast. And he felt odd. His body didn't feel right at all. And then he knew why. His body was small, very small, and it wasn't . . . it wasn't a boy's body any more. He still had two legs, but no arms. Instead, he had wings. He still had two eyes and a mouth, but no nose. Instead, he had a beak. His body was not thin and covered in skin – it was plump, and covered in feathers! He'd been turned into a bird! A little bird, perching in a golden cage!

He opened his mouth – no, his beak – to shout, to scream, to cry. But the only sound that came out was the warble of a bird. He tried to run, but found he could only hop. Inside, he still felt like a boy – like Thomas – but outside, he was a bird.

'Perfect!' said the Ariel, coming closer to him. He looked very big now to the small creature that was Thomas, the eyes like boulders, the mouth like a cave. Bird-Thomas cowered down on his perch, trembling.

'That'll do nicely,' said the Ariel, beaming – his teeth like tombstones – 'for the moment. Now then, I'd best get a move on, or they'll be sending out search parties too quickly.'

He reached a finger through the bars of the cage, and gave a low whistle. Instantly, a feather detached itself from Thomas's side and floated to the Ariel's finger. It hurt Thomas, like a sharp sting. In his bird's voice, he yelped – or tried to. It came out like a croak. The Ariel laughed.

'Dear me, you don't make a very tuneful songbird,' he said. A wild fury filled Thomas to bursting. He hated that Ariel, with all his heart. He wished he could turn him into a cockroach so he could stamp on him!

The Ariel turned away from the cage, back to

the shadow, still held in its globe of light. He reached into the light and gently placed the feather on the shadow's head. He began to hum, a low, tuneful hum that seemed to fill the room. As Thomas stared, the shadow began to change. First of all, it changed colour – the thick black receding, slowly, turning paler, lighter, till it was the colour of Thomas's own skin and clothes. Then, features began to appear – eyes, a nose, a mouth, hair sprouting on the shadow's head, fingers, feet ... Then, the features began to fill in with colour, Thomas's eye colour, and his hair, till the shadow was just like Thomas – or like Thomas had been. It was as perfect as a reflection – but it was unmoving. Then the Ariel blew on it, gently, and all at once it trembled, shook, and began to move.

'You have the strength of my spirit in you now, shadow-child, and the heart of my magic, and it will help you, all the way,' he whispered. 'You will become True Tom, and you will do what I say.'

The shadow-boy's head nodded, up, down, up, down. The eyes moved in their sockets, the limbs shook, the shadow-boy turned his head to look around him, and stared at the Ariel, who smiled.

'You look good, my spirit-child,' he crooned, gently. 'There's just one more thing. A voice.' He touched the shadow-boy's throat, and suddenly, there was Thomas's voice, sounding just slightly different, like a tape-recording, saying, 'Where am I? What's happened?'

'You got lost,' said the Ariel. 'You wandered down a side alley, near the bakers' quarter.'

'I got lost. I wandered down a side alley, near the bakers' quarter,' echoed Shadow-Thomas, while Bird-Thomas hopped up and down on his perch, anxiously.

'You found your way into the heart of the city. Suddenly you overheard people talking. All right so far?'

No! thought Bird-Thomas, in anguish; but Shadow-Thomas nodded and said in his tape-recording voice, 'I overheard people talking.'

'They said Euryon had been spotted, very close by. They said he was looking for special prey, not just the usual Ariel, but something rich and rare – like a Rymer, perhaps. Shaken, you went up to them and asked them for directions to the palace. They told you. One of them – me – actually took you there. And there you told your friends what I've just said.'

'And there I told my friends what you just said,' said Shadow-Thomas, robotically. Bird-Thomas thought, defiantly, Ha, the stupid thing, it has no mind of its own! It will be found out at once!

'And you will agree when I tell your friends you must all go home at once, that it's too dangerous to hang around, that the flying huntsman is nearby, hunting for prey, and that he might find a Rymer hard to resist. Do you understand?'

'Yes, yes, I understand,' said Shadow-Thomas, his Thomas-coloured eyes somehow not as bright as Thomas's own, but alike enough to fool most people.

Oh, no! thought Bird-Thomas, frightened. They really will think it's me, and take the shadow-me home, and leave the real me here, in this cage . . . and I'll never never go back home, never see Dad and Pinch and Patch or anyone again . . .

If a bird could cry, he would have cried then. But he couldn't, and so instead he lifted his head and gave a long, sad whistle. But nobody took any notice. The Ariel was walking with Shadow-Thomas to the door, without a look behind him at poor Bird-Thomas drooping in the cage. In a second, the door slammed, footsteps sounded down the stairs, and Thomas was left quite alone.

FIVE

Pinch and Patch were worried sick. Despite a thorough search of the area by the Duke's men, not a trace had been found of Thomas. Everyone in the bakers' quarter had been questioned, but nobody had seen anything, except for a young woman who said she had been setting out more cakes in her display when she saw Thomas on the other side of the alley, near the entrance to a side passage. 'His back was to me, and he was bending down, looking at something on the road,' she said. She had turned away herself, to arrange a cake properly on a stand, and when she next looked, he had gone. 'I thought he had just walked away,' she said. 'I had no idea anything was wrong.'

That was the only clue. The young woman was questioned, thoroughly, several times, but she couldn't remember anything more than that. At first, the Duke's men seemed to think she might have had something to do with Thomas's disappearance, but it was soon clear that was very far from the case. As to the flying huntsman, there was no evidence at all that he was anywhere near the city yet. Back in the palace, the adults talked together in worried voices while the twins sat nervously around, trying to work out what had happened. Pinch was still convinced the flying huntsman had something to do with it; Patch wasn't so sure. She whispered, 'I've heard there's so much strong magic in Seraphimia that sometimes bits left over from spells hang around in foggy clumps and suck strangers in . . .'

'Don't,' said Pinch, with a shudder. That's almost worse than the flying huntsman.' He leaned forward and hissed in Patch's ear, 'I

don't think much of the Duke, do you?'

Patch agreed. Duke Nimbus *looked* impressive – tall and broad and handsome with a lion's mane of golden hair and bright blue eyes. He wore golden robes and pure white wings sprouted from his big shoulders. But he was vain – he kept glancing at himself in the mirror – and he seemed stupid. Or maybe he was just distracted – but by what? You'd think the disappearance of his guest might be important to him!

It was clear Angelica and the others felt frustrated, and poor Cumulus most of all. He felt responsible, not only for the fact Thomas had vanished, but also because the Duke was so hopeless, and he felt bad about that, because he was a fellow Ariel. Nimbus was only new to the job. His uncle had been Duke before him – and a very good one. But Nimbus wasn't anything like him. Luckily, the Duke's main adviser, Count Cirrus, was a clever man. It was the Count who was doing most of the talking now, while the Duke yawned and looked at his nails.

'I think we should go back on our own to the bakers' quarter and try to retrace Thomas's footsteps,' whispered Patch.

Pinch stared at her. 'They'll never let us go on our own. Not after what happened.'

'We won't tell them. We'll just slip out.'

'Yes, and what if the huntsman gets us too?

Or that fog thing of yours?'

'Well, then we'll have to try and get out of it.'

'Ha, that's easily said.'

'Well,' said Patch, glaring at him and folding her arms, 'do you just want to just sit there like a stranded fish, or do you want to help?'

'Of course I want to help,' said Pinch, 'but . . .'

'But nothing. I'm going to go now. You can come if you want to. Or stay, if you're scared.'

'As if I'd let a girl go on her own,' said Pinch, haughtily.

Keeping an eye on the adults, who were still busy talking, they got up and began to sidle out of the room. There were guards at the door, but Patch whispered to them, in an embarassed sort of voice, 'I'm sorry, but Pinch and me, we really have to *go* – you know. To the bathroom,' she added, hopping up and down on one foot.

'Sure, sure,' said the guard. 'Third door down the corridor.'

They scampered off in that direction. When they got to the bathroom door, they looked behind them. The guards weren't watching. So they ran past the bathroom, and turned the corner into the next corridor.

The palace was a maze of corridors, running off each other. Pinch and Patch hurried along. At last, they found a door which led into a courtyard, and from there, into a walled garden. They scrambled up the wall and looked down into a narrow alley that ran alongside a wide canal. 'Let's jump down and find someone to direct us to the bakers' quarter,' said Patch.

No sooner said than done. They hurried along the alley and soon came across an old lady. 'It's quite a long way,' she said. 'Lots of alleys and streets to go in and out of . . . It would be much quicker if you went by boat. There are gondolas for hire, down there . . .' She pointed to a wharf a little distance away. 'It doesn't cost much.'

'But we haven't any money,' blurted out Pinch. The old lady – an elegant old woman, with silvery hair and a greenish face – looked at him, curiously. 'Dearie me, did you think they'd *give* you the cakes, child? Is that what they do in your country?'

'No, we—' began Pinch, but Patch quelled him with a glare.

'We didn't *think*, you see, madam,' she said, meekly. 'We're visitors from Middler country. Our . . . our parents are out at a conference. We were bored. We thought we'd go exploring. And we have heard so much about the famous bakers' quarter. Now I suppose we'd better go back and . . .'

'No, wait,' said the old lady. Smiling, she fished in her pocket, and took out a couple of small, bright coins. She handed them to Patch. 'Here you are, children. One coin for the boat. Another for a cake each. Have fun. And don't tell too many fibs next time.' And she was off, walking away before they

53

could even thank her.

'That was a nice lady,' said Patch.

'And that was some unbelievable story,' said Pinch, grinning.

'Well, it worked, anyhow, even if she didn't believe it,' retorted Patch. 'Come on, Pinch, let's go and get ourselves a boat!'

The gondolier was a small, surly, wizened Ariel with bat-like wings. He didn't even speak to the twins when they asked him to take them quickly to the bakers' quarter, just grunted and nodded, motioning them to jump into his boat. Then he picked up his pole and pulled away with strong smooth strokes, and soon the gondola was flying lightly along the canal. The twins sat back against the cushions of the boat, and watched the cloudy stream gliding under them, and the houses jostling along the canal.

'It looks different, from here,' said Patch.

'Yes,' said Pinch. 'Sort of sinister.'

'As if those houses are watching us, with their windows like lots of eyes,' said Patch. 'I'm not sure I like it here, are you?'

'No,' said Pinch. 'I always wanted to come here, but now I wish we'd never come.'

Now they were in another canal, narrower than the first, with great tall houses towering over it, and a little white bridge over it. Under the bridge they went, into another canal, wider now, and then to a set of stone steps leading down into the water. The gondolier pulled up there. He pointed up. 'Bakers' quarter,' he said, briefly, and held out a hand. Patch dropped a coin into it. The boatman shook his head. 'Not enough,' he said.

'But the lady said one coin was enough . . .' began Patch.

The gondolier shook his head again. 'You wanted quick. You got quick. You pay,' he growled.

There was nothing for it. They had to give him the other coin. Once they were safely out

of the boat and up the steps, Pinch muttered, 'What a crook!'

'You can say that again,' said Patch, annoyed. 'Now we won't have any money to get a gondola back.'

'Least of our worries,' said Pinch. 'We've got to find Thomas first. Now, I reckon we should start with Signora Anafiela's shop, don't you?'

Signora Anafiela recognised them at once. She fluttered around them, wringing her hands. 'Your poor young friend! I was so shocked when they told me he was missing! Of course I'll help – ask me any questions you like.'

'Er . . . do you think the flying huntsman's got him?' said Pinch.

'What? Of course not. Euryon cannot set foot in our city. It's impossible.'

'Really?'

'Quite, quite impossible,' said Anafiela, firmly.

'But what if he's got an agent in here?'

'An agent?' said Signora Anafiela, and she laughed. 'Euryon always works alone. He'd kill any Ariel foolish enough to think he could work with him. You can put him out of your mind, children. I'm sure it's not him. Besides, he's not anywhere near the city yet. The alarm bells ring when he gets close. They certainly haven't rung yet.'

'Then what if Thomas got lost in a magic fog?' tried Patch.

'That's possible but there was no such fog around at the time, and besides I haven't heard of such a thing happening in any recent time – and I'm no youngster.'

'Then someone must have snatched him,' said Pinch. 'Someone from the city.'

'No Ariel would do such a thing,' said Anafiela, firmly. 'It is against all our laws to snatch an honoured guest. An Ariel who broke such a code would face severe punishment, and be exiled for ever from our lands. Who would try it?'

'Are there only Ariels who live here?' asked Patch.

The baker frowned. 'Yes, if you mean permanently. Nobody else can breathe our air for very long. There are always a few visitors, of course. But they'd all be registered at the visitors' centre and checked up on. It's a long time since we had any troublesome visitors.'

'No Uncouthers?'

'Certainly not! They are banned from Ariel country, you should know that.'

Patch tried another tack.

'The people who were in the shop when we came in this morning, did you know them all?'

Anafiela puffed herself up indignantly. 'You surely aren't suggesting that my customers . . .'

'No, no,' said Patch, hastily, 'it's just that I wondered . . . er . . . whether Thomas got snatched because he's a Rymer, you know, and Cumulus mentioned he was a Rymer when we were here, and . . .'

'Young lady,' said Anafiela, very crossly, 'all

of my customers are good people. They were glad to see a Rymer here! As if they'd do anything to him! And if you keep asking those sorts of questions, I'm afraid I won't be able to help you. Insulting my customers, indeed!'

'Patch didn't mean that . . . I'm sure we think they are a very fine lot of people,' said Pinch, quickly, as his sister seemed lost for words. 'They have very good taste, too.'

Anafiela smiled, pleased. She took the hint, and handed them each a cake. 'Yes, they're a very fine lot, my regular customers. Very clever people, and all Ariels of very good family. There's the wizard Magister Mutandis, and the star-reader Augustus Astrolir and the spell-maker Hecate Longnose and the bird-breeder Colomba Whitewings and the cloud-builder Stratos Pheros . . .' She spoke with great reverence, as if the twins would know all these names. They didn't, of course; but they listened, all the same, and filed the names away in their heads.

Through a mouthful of cake, Pinch said, 'Do your regular customers live nearby, Signora?'

'One or two. Others are more far-flung.'

'Does the wizard – I mean, Magister Mutandis – does he live close by?'

'No. He lives on the other side of the square, not far from the palace. So do Augustus Astrolir and Hecate Longnose.'

The wizard, the star-reader and the spell-maker, thought the twins. Well, of those three, the first and last seemed the most likely to be involved. Of course, the baker had said no Ariel could possibly be involved – but could you really be sure of that? There were bad people everywhere, and not just in Uncouther country.

After thanking Anafiela very politely, the twins left the shop. But they did not head to the square straight away. Instead, they walked up and down the alley, sniffing the air, trying to work out exactly how Thomas might have been snatched, and ignoring the interested looks of the other shopkeepers, peering through their windows.

'I mean, one moment he was here, the next he wasn't,' said Pinch, thoughtfully. 'And there was no one else there. I mean, no other person, except us.'

'Perhaps the kidnapper made himself invisible,' suggested Patch.

'Yes! Maybe he was waiting outside, invisible – or he followed us, invisibly. He came up to Thomas when we weren't looking, and put him under a spell.'

'I know! Maybe he thinned Thomas,' cried Patch.

'Maybe. Or maybe he turned him into a pebble and put it into his pocket.'

'A *pebble?*'

'Well, you know, I'm only guessing. Anyway, somehow he got past us. Maybe he even just walked through a wall.'

'Lots of maybes,' said Patch. 'But I'm sure Thomas was taken because he's a Rymer. And lots of people knew he was a Rymer. Not just the people at the shop, but also Duke Nimbus and his staff and also the visitors' centre and just about anyone you can think of.'

'Well, Signora Anafiela didn't know before Cumulus told her,' said Pinch. 'I'm sure of that. And neither did those customers, I bet. I think that person took Thomas on the spur of the moment. This wasn't planned.'

'We can't be sure of that. Maybe it was a well-made plan. Maybe Duke Nimbus agreed to our visit because he actually was planning to have Thomas snatched.'

'Don't be silly, Patch,' said Pinch, scornfully. 'Why would he do that? That would cause a huge fuss. The Ariels don't want trouble with our country. No, I really think it's something to do with one of those customers.'

'But why would they take him?'

Pinch shrugged. 'I don't know.'

'Signora Anafiela said Ariels wouldn't be involved in such a . . .'

Pinch snorted. 'As if! There are plenty of Ariel crooks, I bet – just think of that boatman.'

Patch grinned. 'Right. But that still doesn't explain why they'd want to take him.'

'Maybe they want something from him. Maybe they want to experiment on him . . .'

'Don't,' shuddered Patch.

'Or maybe they want to do what the flying huntsman does, and ransom him. I don't know. But I think we've got to go and talk to those customers – somehow without making them suspicious.'

'Somehow!' said Patch, with feeling.

'I think we should go to their houses and knock on the door. Well, one of us knocks and the other hides – maybe turns into a frog and hides in the other one's pocket. The one who knocks – that could be me – asks if that person is there. If they are, I just say I've heard a lot about them, and can I have their autograph? Magicians are always vain. They'll let us in, I bet, and while I'm talking, you, as a frog, can have a snoop around.'

'And if they aren't there?'

'Well, we both turn into frogs, get into the house somehow, and snoop around.'

'*Frogs*,' snorted Patch. 'Insects would be better. That way it's easy to get into the houses – we can even squeeze in through keyholes.'

'Hope no one swats us, then,' grumbled Pinch, but he couldn't say any more, for he didn't have any better ideas.

SIX

Thomas sat listlessly in his cage, his bird-head sunk down on his bird-chest. He had lost hope. He had tried to remember every spell, every magic formula, all the glamouring and pishogue he'd seen and heard in Owlchurch and in other places of the Hidden World. But he couldn't remember anything which would change his shape back from bird to boy. In fact, he could hardly remember anything much at all. He felt as if his mind was beginning to crumble. Maybe soon even my mind will turn into a bird-brain, he thought. Maybe then I'll even forget I'm Thomas Trew. I'll just think I'm a silly little plump bird sitting in a golden cage. I'll just sit here and warble and sing, and little by little I'll forget Dad's waiting for me, and my friends will take that shadow-creature home, and everyone will think it's me, and so no one will miss me . . .

With an effort, he drew himself up. I must not give up, he told himself sternly. I must not give up. I must not give up!

He said the last one out loud, and though it came out as a kind of twittering, he almost felt he could hear the words in it. So he said it again, and this time it was sharper, the words a little clearer. Once more; and suddenly, a voice answered him. It was a small, but very sharp voice, and it said, 'Giving up is the last thing you should do.'

'What?' said Thomas, and the word came out like a croak.

The voice repeated, 'I said, giving up is the last thing you should do.'

They were words – definitely words. But Thomas couldn't see anyone, though he peered everywhere with his beady bird's eyes.

'Down below you, to the left on the skirting-board,' said the voice. Thomas hopped down from his perch and putting his head to one side, tried to peer through the bars, down to his left. He could see the skirting-board now.

'The knot-hole,' said the sharp voice. 'See it? See me?'

Thomas could see – just – a little knot-hole in the skirting-board, and there – was that a shine, a glitter? A round eye, pressed to the opening!

'Who . . . who are you?' he warbled.

'Ratshaun O'Rattus,' said the voice, promptly. As Thomas watched, a little creature emerged from the knot-hole – a small, sleek black rat, with bright eyes and long whiskers and tail. Its whiskers twitched. It sat on its haunches and looked up at Thomas. 'Ratty for short,' it went on. 'I came to this dratted city on a bit of a holiday – well, to tell you the truth, I hitched an illegal ride in an Ariel sun-sailor – always wanted to pilot one of those, you know – but just minutes after landing, I got scooped up by our nasty friend Four Eyes.'

'Who?'

'The Ariel sorcerer or whatever he is. He just snatched me, you know, brought me here, turned me into a rat, but forgot rats can run pretty quickly. I saw the knot-hole, dived in. He hasn't been able to catch me. Guess that's why he caught you instead. You didn't get away quickly enough.'

'But why? Why does he want us?'

'No idea,' said the rat. 'Some horrid plot, I imagine – maybe he wants to make a really potent spell from our bones or something. Or maybe he's just practising his magic on us. But anyway, where are you from? What's your name?'

'Thomas,' said Thomas, his heart beating fast. 'My name's Thomas. Thomas Trew. I'm a human – a Rymer. I've been living in Owlchurch, in Middler country, with my friends.'

Ratty gave a low whistle. 'Wow! A human – and a Rymer at that! I'm not anything exotic like that. I'm a Middler, though, from a little place not far from Arkadia.'

'Arkadia?' said Thomas. 'I've been there.*

'Really? Not a bad place, eh? Wish old Pan could help us now, don't you?'

'Yes,' said Thomas, sadly.

'Fact is, he can't,' said Ratty, cheerfully. 'So we've got to get out of this pickle ourselves, eh?'

'I can't. But you can,' said Thomas. 'You're a Middler – you must know magic. I can't remember any of the stuff I was taught.'

'Well,' said Ratty, 'trouble is, the magic he's

* In *Thomas Trew and the Horns of Pan*.

70

used to transform us is so strong that you can't just break it with a counter-spell from the lands below. You've either got to find another Ariel spell that will counteract it or, better still, a spell even stronger than that.'

'Stronger than that?'

'One from the beginning of time, from the morning of the world,' said Ratty.

Thomas thought the words sounded familiar, but he couldn't think why for the moment. Instead, he said, 'What can we do, then?'

'We've got to get someone to get us a spell like that. I mean – you can't go anywhere, being as you're a bird in a cage, and I *could* go somewhere, being a rat in a hole – but on the other hand, people run after rats with brooms, even up here, and I might well get a big lump on my noggin for my trouble if I try and get an Ariel to help us. Besides, Four Eyes has fixed it so that only metamorphs can understand us, and not ordinary people.'

'Metamorphs?' said Thomas, faintly.

'People who have been turned into animals and things,' said Ratty, briskly. 'So you see that's why I can understand your warbling and you can understand my squeaking. But no one else can. Except Four Eyes, of course.'

'Oh dear,' said Thomas.

'Oh dear is right,' said Ratty. 'But never say die, is my motto. We'll find a way, young Thomas. Never you fret.'

'Right,' said Thomas. 'Do you have any ideas?'

'I already told you my idea,' said Ratty, shiftily. 'What about yours?'

'Er – I think I've got to get out of this cage. Then I can fly out of the window and go looking for help.'

'Hey, that's excellent!' cried Ratty, brightly. 'Nobody will go after *you* with a broom! And you can always land on some nice Ariel's shoulder, or go winging around looking for a metamorph to help us . . . yes, I like it!' He put his head on one side and stared up at Thomas. 'Well – how are you going to do it?'

'You're going to help me,' said Thomas. 'By gnawing through the bars.'

'Are you crazy? I'll break my teeth! Those bars are gold!'

'You're a Middler,' said Thomas. 'You know pishogue. Don't you know a bit that might help?'

'Well . . . my speciality is tricks, really, so I—'

'You're a Trickster?' cut in Thomas. 'Like Hinkypunk Hobthrust, in my village?'

'Well, not quite as good as him. I've heard of him, yes. Pretty amazing, so I'm told. No, me, I'm a kind of minor Trickster – a leprechaun, to be precise.'

'Oh! I've never met a leprechaun before.'

'Well, now you have – in a manner of speaking, given as this is not my true shape.'

'What sorts of tricks do leprechauns have, then?'

'Not the kind to make me gnaw through gold,' said Ratty, firmly. 'And anyway I don't have my bag of tricks with me. I need it to do proper pishogue.'

Thomas was exasperated. 'But you must know some by heart! What about a trick that might make the bars vanish – or make them open – or bend them so I can squeeze out . . . or . . .'

'Wait, wait,' said Ratty, hopping up and down with excitement. 'I just thought of something! Something that doesn't need my bag of tricks. It might work or it might not, but I can try. Now . . . hmm . . . let me see . . . if I jump on to the table . . . yes – like so – then reach out to the cage – hmm, still can't reach it . . . maybe if I balance on that book, there – and spring across . . .'

He suited the action to the word. The cage swung wildly on its stand as the rat landed on top of it. Thomas was flung about. He squeaked, 'Careful, you'll get me squashed against the bars!'

'Sorry,' said Ratty. He waited till the cage stopped swinging, then scrambled down from the and top and, hanging like an acrobat, reached for the door at the bottom. He grinned in at Thomas, showing some very sharp white teeth.

'Soon have you out, birdy,' he said, and then he blew on the bars, very hard. He said, 'Peacock I hold, peacock I'm told . . .'

At first, nothing happened. Then all at once, the door began to grow. It grew and grew, and the bars grew with it. Up, up they stretched, getting thicker and taller – and as they did so, the gap between the bars grew wider, and wider, until pretty soon, they were wide enough for Thomas to fly through. He fluttered out, rather weakly, landing on top of a pile of books. Ratty grinned at him. 'Good, eh?' he said, and then he turned back to the cage, and blew on the door once more. He said, 'Sparrow I hold, sparrow I'm told.' At once, it began to shrink, faster and faster, till soon it was the same size it had been, and the bars with it.

'That was amazing!' said Thomas. 'What?'

'I tricked the cage into thinking it housed

a peacock, not a sparrow or whatever it is you are,' said Ratty, casually grooming his whiskers.

'Oh. I see. No. I don't. How can you trick a cage? It can't think anything at all.'

'In your world,' said Ratty. 'But then in your world, do boys get turned into birds? Anyway, the cage doesn't exactly *think*. It's programmed . . .'

'Like a computer,' said Thomas.

'Whatever that is. As I was saying, the cage was programmed by the spell Four Eyes put on it – to hold the bird. My trick didn't *break* the spell – it only modified it, slightly. "Hold the bird" became "Hold the big bird". So the cage had to change, you see.'

'Very clever,' said Thomas.

'Well, I like tinkering with machines,' said Ratty, modestly. 'Mind you, that sort of thing doesn't always work. But this time it did, lucky for us.'

'What I don't understand,' said Thomas, 'is why, if you know magic like that, you got turned into a rat by that man and you can't change back?'

'I told you, that sort of magic is too strong. You can't break it and it's no use trying to modify it – you might just change from a sparrow to a peacock, or a rat to a mouse, and what good would that do you? And he caught me by surprise. It happens even to Tricksters, you know. Maybe not to your Hinkypunk, but as I said, I'm not in his class.' He scrambled off the table, and ran up the windowsill. He swung on the latch of the window, and it swung open. 'There. Now, my friend, if I were you, I'd get going, and pretty fast. Four Eyes will be back soon.'

Thomas flew to the windowsill. He paused, looking at the little rat. 'What about you?'

'I'll be right, for the moment. I'll get back in my knot-hole. He can't get me out of there. Just go and find help, OK?' He grinned. 'Imagine how surprised old Four Eyes will be when he comes in and sees the little bird has flown – out of the bars of his cage and into thin air! Good luck, Thomas, and get back quickly, OK?'

'OK,' said Thomas, and he jumped off the windowsill, and into the cool clear air outside.

SEVEN

Pinch and Patch soon found out Magister Mutandis and Hecate Longnose lived in the same street, just off the square. They'd go there first. As they hurried along, Patch said, 'We haven't really thought of just what we're going to do, if we find out who's holding Thomas and where . . .'

'It's no use planning,' said Pinch. 'We don't know what we'll find. I think we play it by ear.'

'Then I hope we don't go deaf,' said Patch, dryly.

Hecate Longnose's house was first. It was rather different to most houses in Seraphimia. It was a tall thin grey house with a peaked roof pulled down over its eaves, rather like a too-big witch's hat. The knocker on the door was shaped like a dragon's head and on the doorstep was a mat which read 'Beware of the Magic', in letters that winked on and off, on and off.

They looked up and down the street. It was quite empty. And nobody appeared to be watching from any windows. 'OK,' said Pinch. 'On the count of three, Patch, turn into something that can sit in my pocket.'

Patch grinned. 'OK.'

'One . . . two . . . three . . .' whispered Pinch, and suddenly, there was a little popping sound, and there on the toe of Pinch's left shoe was a ladybird. The little creature whirred up into the air, landed on Pinch's shoulder, and he heard Patch's voice. 'I can't stay like this for more than half an hour, so you're going to have to hurry,' and then ladybird-Patch flew down from his shoulder into his pocket, where she stayed very quietly.

'OK, OK, let's do it,' said Pinch. He went

boldly up to the door and knocked. A big hollow boom sounded. The dragon's eyes lit up, all red. A deep voice roared, 'Who is it that troubles the repose of Hecate Longnose? State your business, stranger!'

'I'm not troubling anyone, really I'm not,' said Pinch, swallowing. 'I just want . . . I'm a visitor to this city and I've heard so much of Signora Longnose and I wondered if she might sign an autograph for me . . .'

'An autograph?' boomed the voice, in a different tone; then the door opened, wide, and Pinch stepped inside.

It was very dark in there, and smelled odd. Pinch could feel Patch scritch-scratching a little in his pocket; he knew she was nervous too. The door closed behind him with a bang and he thought, Oh, no, what if we're trapped?

But it was too late to think again, because just then the light came on, blindingly, and the deep voice boomed, right in Pinch's ear, it seemed, 'Here I am and here you are, and now tell me what you really want.'

Pinch jumped. 'I . . . I want an autograph,' he said, turning to face Hecate Longnose. But there he got a surprise. For the owner of that deep voice and that tall thin house was a little dumpy woman, rather like Signora Anafiela, with bright eyes and a long nose and moth-wings of the same kind as the baker's, but with a different pattern on it, that reminded you vaguely of a skull.

'Signora Longnose . . .' Pinch began.

'No, no, no,' said the little woman, 'no more fibs, and tell me why you've come here to snoop.' Her bright eyes fixed Pinch with a glare. 'Don't you know I could turn you into a rat or a beetle or anything I care to, just with a word?'

'We're Middlers,' squeaked Pinch, quite losing his head, 'you can't do—'

'We, eh?' said Hecate, with a grim smile. 'Where's the other, hmm? Your twin? Your sister?'

'I'm here,' said Patch, scrambling out of the

pocket as the ladybird but turning back into a girl the moment she hit the ground. 'I'm here and don't you try anything, Pinch and I know lots of tricks!'

'Well, well,' said Hecate, 'feisty little thing, aren't you?' Her currant eyes shone mischievously. 'I'm sure you don't know as many as I do, little Middler, but no mind. I know you. I saw you in Anafiela's shop this morning. With your friend. Is he with you?'

Pinch and Patch stared at her.

'Oh dear, haven't you heard?' said Patch. Pinch shot her a meaningful look. If Hecate didn't even know Thomas had vanished, she'd likely know nothing at all. They should get on to Magister Mutandis's house.

Hecate frowned and said, 'Heard what?'

'Thomas was snatched, and—'

'Oh, no, dear.' Hecate shook her head, decisively. 'He just got lost. At least, that's what I heard he said.'

'Whatever do you mean?' cried the twins, together.

'I heard it on the way home from the markets,' said Hecate. 'Your friend – Thomas, was it? – was found wandering in the square and was taken back to the palace. Odd. But true.'

'When?' shouted Pinch.

'Why, maybe twenty minutes ago,' said Hecate, puzzled.

She was even more puzzled when they turned and ran for the door, wrenched it open, and fell out into the street. 'Young people these days,' she muttered to herself, as she stumped off to her kitchen, 'no manners at all, and quite, quite mad.'

The young people in question ran as fast as their legs could carry them, back to the palace. At the main door, they asked the guards if Thomas was really back.

'Why, yes,' said one of the guards. 'Just a little while ago. He's in the audience chamber with your people, and Count Cirrus, the Duke's adviser, is . . .'

Without waiting to hear any more, Pinch and Patch ran through the endless corridors till they reached the audience chamber. They burst in, puffing and panting. Everyone turned to look at them, in surprise.

Angelica said, 'Wherever have you been? We all wondered . . .'

But Pinch and Patch had no eyes or ears for her. They were staring at Thomas, who stood facing the Duke, between Adverse and a stranger they had never seen before. He was a tall thin Ariel in plain robes, with tousled hair and a vague, friendly face, mild blue eyes behind big spectacles. Ragged grey wings protruded from his robes.

'Why, these must be your friends, Thomas,' the man said, turning to the twins, with a friendly smile.

But Thomas did not turn around. The Ariel touched him lightly on the shoulder. 'Thomas, your friends,' he repeated.

This time, Thomas turned. He stared at Pinch and Patch. 'Oh, hello,' he said, weakly. 'I'm really pleased to see you.'

'And so are we,' said Patch, warmly.

'Oh, Thomas, what happened?' cried Pinch.

'I got lost,' whispered Thomas.

'But how? Where did you go? Why didn't people see you?'

'Oh, but they did,' said the stranger, gently. 'Once he'd emerged in the square, that is. You see, children, it can be hard to find your way, in our city.'

Pinch and Patch said nothing. *They'd* managed well enough. They looked at Thomas. He was not looking well, Patch thought. He looks peaky, thought Pinch. Something's happened.

The stranger was watching them. 'I'm afraid Thomas has had a shock,' he said. 'He overheard people saying that the flying huntsman was after a Rymer.'

'The flying huntsman!' said Pinch. 'We thought he'd got you, Thomas.'

'Did you?' said the stranger, sharply. Then he smiled. 'It's all right. Euryon won't be here till tonight at the earliest. I've seen his path, in my telescope.'

'Signor Astrolir is our most distinguished star-reader,' explained Count Cirrus, speaking for the first time. 'In his studies, he can plot the paths that giants like Euryon make through the sky.'

'And we are greatly indebted to you, sir, for bringing Thomas safely back,' said Angelica, bowing to Signor Astrolir.

'We certainly are,' echoed Cumulus, heartily. He was looking very relieved indeed.

'My pleasure,' said the star-reader, bowing and smiling. 'It was a small enough thing to do.'

'But now, we have to go,' said Angelica.

'We have to get Thomas home,' added Adverse. 'There's no time to lose.'

'We'll send an escort with you,' said Count

87

Cirrus, 'a party of armed sun-sailors to make sure there's no ambush. Duke Nimbus said to spare no expense.'

'Do thank him for us,' said Angelica, briskly.

'He would have liked to farewell you, but the Montaynard Ambassador has just arrived and he does stand on ceremony. We will, of course, be happy to welcome you once again when the danger's past. We . . .'

Under the cover of Count Cirrus's talk, Pinch and Patch sidled up to Thomas.

'Are you OK?' Pinch whispered.

Thomas jumped. He mumbled, 'Yes.'

'Don't worry,' said Astrolir, leaning towards them, confidingly. 'He's had a bit of a shock. Panicked when he knew he was lost, lost his head a bit. And then, hearing those people talking about the flying huntsman . . . well, it's no wonder he's feeling scared.'

Patch looked at him. She wished he wouldn't speak for Thomas. She said, 'Are you scared?'

He looked down, and nodded, miserably.

Pinch said, eagerly, 'Don't you worry, Thomas, we won't let that flying huntsman get you! You heard Count Cirrus – they're sending armed ships to escort us home.'

'And in any case Euryon won't be around till at least tonight,' put in Astrolir, smoothly. 'You'll be fine, Thomas.'

'Yes,' said Thomas, and he smiled in a rather watery sort of way.

At that moment, Adverse came over to them. 'In all the hubbub, you two rascals never explained where you went off to like that,' he said, rather accusingly. 'What did you think you were doing?'

'Well—' began Pinch, but Patch cut in.

'Actually Pinch wanted another of those moon-cakes so we went looking for that bakery,' she said. 'We thought it was closer than it really was.'

Adverse sighed. 'What a time to be greedy!' he said. 'Really, Pinch, you could control yourself.'

'But I didn't—' began poor Pinch, but Patch trod on his toe. 'Ow!' he shouted. 'That hurt!'

'OK, children, no more horseplay,' said Angelica, briskly, as Pinch glared at his sister. 'Off we go. Oh, dear, wait, forgive my bad manners . . .' She held out a hand to Astrolir. 'Thank you again, Signor Astrolir, for bringing Thomas safely back to us.'

'It was nothing,' said Astrolir. 'Anyone would have done the same. Well, I hope you have a good trip, and let's hope we see you again up here soon?'

'Not too soon, I'll warrant,' said Angelica, rather grimly. 'But I hope you might come for a visit to us?'

'I should like that,' said the star-reader, beaming. 'Good day to you, all, and safe trip.' He reached over to Thomas, looking down into his eyes. 'And my dear Thomas, take care. Take *very* great care. Now, if you'll excuse me, I really must get back to my telescope.' And he was off, with a brisk step, turning once to wave at them.

'A kind man,' said Angelica, 'and a helpful one.'

'Very helpful,' said Thomas, quietly. Pinch and Patch were puzzled by the expression in his eyes. Was it fear?

'OK, it's all set,' said Count Cirrus, coming towards them. 'The sun-sailors are ready to escort you. Will you take my arm, Signora?'

With Count Cirrus and Angelica in the lead, they set off, Pinch and Patch and Thomas in the rear of the party. Now was the time to talk, thought the twins, and find out what had happened, and what Thomas was keeping back. For they were sure he was keeping back *something* . . . Of all the people there, they knew him best of all, and they were surprised by the way he'd reacted to what was surely just an ordinary sort of adventure, a mishap really.

'We're so glad you're back! I thought the flying huntsman had already got you,' said

Pinch, brightly. 'And Patch thought it was magic fog. Or that you'd got snatched by someone. We never dreamed you just got lost.'

'Well, I did,' said Thomas.

'Yes, but people looked for you everywhere . . .'

'It's a big place. And I'm small.'

'That's true, but this lady, one of the bakers, she said she saw you stop in the street and bend down to look at something, and—'

'And what?' snapped Thomas. 'So what if she saw me? It must have been just before I got lost. It's not you that got lost. It's me. You don't know what it's like. So why don't you just shut up and leave me alone?'

The twins goggled at him. Patch said, quietly, 'Sorry, Thomas. We didn't mean . . .'

But Thomas had stalked off, after the others.

'What's bitten him?' said Pinch.

'I don't know,' said Patch. She stared after him – and in that instant saw something that at first made no sense. No sense at all. She frowned.

Pinch said, 'Maybe all the magic around in this city has made him queasy or crazy or something so he's not really himself, and . . .'

Patch stopped dead. She whispered, 'Pinch. Wait.'

'What for?'

'There's something – something I don't quite understand.'

'Lots of things I don't understand,' said Pinch. 'Not a reason for hanging around.' The others had already gone out, Thomas at their heels. 'Look, what's up, Patch?'

Patch was looking thoughtfully into a mirrored panel on the wall. 'Pinch, come here.'

'Why? What are you doing?'

'Can you see me?'

'Have you gone nutty too? Of course I can see you.'

'In the mirror, I mean.'

'Well, now,' said Pinch, sarcastically, 'I think I do, you know. It's called a reflection, Patch. Haven't you heard about—'

'Shut up, Pinch. I didn't see *him*, that's the thing.'

Pinch hit his forehead with his hand. 'You *have* gone nutty! What are you talking about?'

'Pinch – when Thomas walked past that mirror just before – I didn't see his reflection.'

Pinch stared. 'What?'

'I thought at first that maybe because it was an Ariel mirror it might only reflect Ariels. But that's not true. We can see ourselves in it too. And I saw all the others.'

'Well, maybe it doesn't reflect humans,' said Pinch. 'I mean we're all from the Hidden World. Only Thomas isn't.'

'That's true,' said Patch, a bit crestfallen.

'Look, Patch,' said Pinch, 'we're all in a hurry and we can't just hang around so we can check mirrors and things. But I'm sure that's the explanation.'

'You're probably right,' said Patch. 'But just for a moment, I thought maybe he had a spell on him or something . . . I thought . . . oh well, never mind. I guess I'm just a bit miffed. Thomas isn't being very nice, is he?'

'No,' said Pinch, 'but he'll be OK, soon, I expect. It's like Astrolir said – he's had a shock. A bad experience.'

'He's had worse experiences before and not been like this,' said Patch, stubbornly. 'What about when he fell into Uncouther country? What about when we got kidnapped? What about when Pan got angry? Or the Syren, trying to—'

'Look, I don't know. Fact is, he's taken it like that this time. Nothing we can do,' said Pinch, impatiently. 'Come on, Patch, or we'll be in big trouble if we keep them waiting.'

EIGHT

I t had all seemed so clear to Thomas, back
in his prison. He would escape, find
someone who could break the spell, and
go back to his friends. But now he was out,
flying about in the bright golden air, he wasn't
so sure. It was no use flying straight back to his
friends; they wouldn't understand what he was
saying. Besides, Shadow-Thomas must be with
them, fooling them into believing he was the
real Thomas. What was more, Ratty had said
only an Ariel counter-spell would help him, or
one from what was it, 'the beginning of time,
morning of the world'? Whatever that was. But
who should he try? He knew no one in this
city, except for the baker, Signora Anafiela,

and she dealt in cakes, not spells. As he flew, he racked his brains, trying to remember exactly how he'd been caught. He'd been in the street – and, yes, that's right, there'd been a little dog – he had reached down to pat it – and boom! Suddenly, he had thinned!

So the dog must either have been the magician himself, or an illusion created by him. Perhaps someone had seen the dog, Thomas thought, hopefully. Perhaps they were already investigating . . . But, no, if they've got Shadow-Thomas, pretending he'd got lost, then they won't know *I'm* still missing, that the real me's not there at all . . . Shadow-Thomas must be a programmed thing, like the cage, like a computer, but also in a funny way, a part of me, like my shadow, like my reflection.

Oh dear, he thought, miserably, this has to be the worst adventure I've ever been in. Worse even than being at the mercy of General Legion Morningstar? Yes, because he hadn't expected anything bad here. The

Uncouthers were the enemies of everyone else in the Hidden World; but the Ariels were supposed to be friends, allies. You expected to be attacked by enemies, not friends.

Why, why, *why* had the Ariel captured him? What had Thomas ever done to him? Was he working alone, or with others? Could he be working with Uncouthers, or *for* them, anyway? They couldn't come up here, but that didn't mean they didn't have agents here, renegade Ariels. In a way, if that was the case, it was more understandable. He knew the Uncouthers hated him. He knew the General and also his secretary, Fustian Jargon, would love to get their own back on him for things he'd done. But if it wasn't an Uncouther plot – if it was just an Ariel thing, who could he really trust in this city? How could he be sure they'd be on his side, and not that man's? And he had no idea what the man could want with him. Well, that wasn't quite true. He had some idea – it could be connected to his being a Rymer.

But in what way, and what use would a Rymer be to him? From what he'd said to Shadow-Thomas, the flying huntsman was much more likely to want a Rymer, to ransom and . . .

His heart fluttered wildly. The flying huntsman! That was where he'd heard that strange phrase, 'the beginning of time, morning of the world'. Cumulus had said the huntsman came from there. He wasn't an Ariel, but a star-giant from the beginning of time, the morning of the world.

At that moment, a strange, dangerous and frightening idea popped into Thomas's head, fully formed and quite unexpected. He nearly fell out of the air in fright at his own thoughts. Are you crazy, Thomas? he scolded himself. Quite, quite mad? That would never work. It would be like jumping from a hot frying-pan to a raging fire. You can't do that. You just can't. Go now and find a friendly Ariel, Signora Anafiela, for instance, and don't do the mad, mad thing that's in your mind. Forget it, in fact.

Forget you even thought of it.

But somehow, though he winged away towards the bakers' quarter, the mad idea stayed in his mind, and it wouldn't leave him alone.

He landed in the alley just near the bakery. A few seconds later, a customer came out of the door, and Bird-Thomas flew right in. He fluttered around the counter, twittering madly.

His arrival caused quite a stir. The baker and her assistant and the customers flapped their hands wildly at him. 'Shoo! Shoo!' A customer opened the door wide so he could fly out, but of course he didn't. He fluttered around in circles, trying to think of something that would make the baker understand what he wanted. Crumbs, he thought, suddenly. I could spell the word HELP out in crumbs. He dived for a tray of little iced cakes and pecked out a large crumb. He brought it back to the counter. He went back to the tray, and got another crumb. Back to the counter, then back to the cakes, pecking out a crumb and . . . But this time, before he could fly away, someone took a swipe at him that he only just escaped from. Frightened out of his wits, choking on the big crumb, he struggled desperately out of the man's hand. Leaving a few feathers behind, he hurtled up into the air. Swallowing the crumb, he twittered wildly, trying hard to make them understand.

'What is the matter with that thing?' said the baker's assistant, puzzled.

'It's mad,' said a customer.

'Flew too close to the sun, I shouldn't wonder,' said another.

But Signora Anafiela's raisin eyes had sharpened, as she watched him circling above her. 'There's something odd about that creature . . . yes – something rather odd. I know! I can't understand it! It can't talk! It's like a bird that's come from goodness knows where – it's not an Ariel bird. Maybe it's a spy.' She turned to her assistant. 'Go and get the net. We'll have to catch him.'

Oh no you don't, thought Thomas, and in a panicked rush, he swooped down and darted to the door. But one of the customers saw him coming, and slammed it before Thomas could escape. He made a grab at Thomas, who shot up into the air, right up to the ceiling, where he hovered, desperately trying to decide what to do.

'Don't be afraid,' crooned the baker, standing on top of a chair and reaching out a hand to him. 'Don't be afraid, little one. We don't want to hurt you, just help you.' Her eyes glistened softly. 'Come on, come down . . .'

No fear, thought Thomas, hovering. What was that up there – a chink of light, in the ceiling . . . was there a hole? Could he squeeze through there? It looked very small but then he was pretty small too . . . Like Ratty squeezing through that knot-hole . . .

The baker's assistant had brought the net. Signora Anafiela flung it towards him. That decided Thomas. He wasn't going to stay here to be caught in that net. He darted over to the chink of light in the corner of the ceiling and threw himself at it. But he hit his head on the ceiling, and, dazed, fell a little way before recovering and shooting up again, just in time to escape the net. He flung himself at the hole again, and this time, managed to get his head and half his body in. Help, he was stuck!

'Stand on my shoulders, Anafiela, you'll reach him that way, he can't get through!' he heard someone shout. With a mighty effort, he heaved and pulled, and quite suddenly, he was through, like a cork popping out of the neck of a bottle.

He was in the roof-space now; it was dusty and very bright. There was a tall narrow silver chimney in the middle of it. Thomas stood quiet for a moment, getting his breath back. He felt sick. There was a funny feeling in his throat. He could hear confused shouts below, and a scraping sound. A ladder, he thought suddenly, I bet they're getting a ladder, there's probably a way of getting up into the roof-space. Yes – there was a trapdoor. Oh, no! He must get out! He fluttered around, trying to find a chink of light – something – anything . . . but he couldn't see a thing. The roof seemed shut up quite tightly. And he was getting so tired. His wings hurt, and his heart was racing madly . . .

He heard a rattle. The trapdoor was lifting up. He had no time! Thomas looked wildly around, hoping to at least hide so they couldn't catch him. Perhaps he could hide in the shadows, and when they opened the door, make a dash for it. But then he'd just be in the shop, and . . .

The flue! The chimney flue went up and up, straight up on to the roof above. Into the air! And the fire wasn't lit, he'd seen that in the shop. He could get out that way. There must be a way of getting into the flue. He flew around it, trying to find the way in.

All at once the trapdoor below him opened

right up. A hand appeared, then a face, and the person began to heave themselves up. In a minute, Thomas would be trapped!

'No, no, no!' he moaned. 'Oh, how I wish I could fly up the chimney and get out!'

No sooner were the words out of his beak than his throat began to swell and swell and swell. It hurt horribly. Just as he thought he'd choke, up came the biggest burp, and with it a puff of silvery smoke. The smoke wreathed around the chimney flue – and then the metal began to shiver and shake. All at once, the chimney slid open. In the next instant, Thomas heard a shout behind him. Without thinking, he dived straight into the opening. Just in time, the chimney closed behind him, and he was in close darkness, his heart racing so hard he thought it might burst out of his chest.

The chimney flue went up and up, dark, narrow, rather choking. But he could see a chink of light up the top now. With the last of his strength, he winged up, up, up. It seemed to take a long time, with his heart bumping and thudding like a drum, and every muscle screaming – but at last he reached the top of the chimney, and flopped out exhausted into the bright shining air.

NINE

They were hovering over the sky-ocean now, weaving their way in and out of the cloud-islands. Nobody spoke much. Even Angelica and Adverse, in the front seat, hardly exchanged a word. Cumulus, meanwhile, had taken a seat in one of the sun-sailors sent to escort them home.

Pinch and Patch tried at first to chat to Thomas. But he didn't want to. He just sat staring out of the window at the fleet of sun-sailors. Not once did he look at the twins. They felt a bit hurt about this, and a little puzzled. It wasn't like Thomas to be so surly. But after all, they felt pretty low too about the way things had turned out. It had been a really disappointing visit.

Suddenly, as they passed a silver tower, its light flashed once, twice, in through Metallicus's windows. Thomas gave a little cry, shrank back, and covered his face.

'What's the matter, Thomas?' hissed Pinch.

Thomas said nothing, just shook his head.

The light flashed once more. Thomas huddled down behind the seat. He was shaking.

'What's up?' said Patch, frightened. She reached out a hand to Thomas, and touched him on the shoulder. She drew back, as if stung. He was so cold that the touch of him burned like ice!

'Pinch,' she whispered, 'I think there's something really wrong with Thomas . . .'

'It's the shock or something,' said Pinch, trying to speak lightly. But inside, he was frightened too. He'd seen something that puzzled and worried him. When the light had flashed the third time, it had lit up the whole car, bathing everyone in unearthly blue-white light, like a huge bolt of lightning. Everyone's shapes had been clearly defined – except for Thomas. In fact, *he had vanished altogether*, just for that tiny instant. The next, there he was again. But it was odd. Very, very odd. He must watch and see if it happened again, or whether he'd been imagining it.

But the flash did not come again. They passed by the cloud-island without anything else happening. Thomas relaxed again and sat back in his usual position on the back seat, staring out of the window at the sun-sailors.

For a little while, the twins watched the sun-sailors too. Normally, it would have been fun, for the golden airships were quite something. You could see their pilots clearly, seated at the clear controls. One of them saw the twins looking at him, and waved, and the twins waved back, feeling their hearts rise again for a moment.

'Aren't the sun-sailors amazing, Thomas?'

said Patch, gently. 'Don't you wish you could ride in them, like Cumulus?'

'No,' said Thomas, sharply.

Hurt, Patch looked at Pinch, who shrugged, helplessly.

'I would like to, though,' said Patch, bravely.

Thomas said nothing.

'*Everyone's* disappointed at leaving like this, so soon,' said Patch, still trying. 'Not just you.'

Thomas said nothing.

'Oh, blow you, if you won't speak to me, then I won't speak to you,' said Patch, crossly.

'Good,' muttered Thomas.

'I don't know what's wrong with you,' snapped Patch. 'You're acting weird. What really happened to you when you got lost?'

For the first time, Thomas turned around. There was a strange glint in his eyes. 'Be quiet, you stupid, meddling little Middler,' he hissed. He leaned towards Patch. His breath puffed coldly over her face. He whispered, 'Shut up, right now – or I'll turn you to stone. I can, you know – if you even try to call for help or warn anyone at all.'

Patch gave a little cry and drew right back. She and Pinch clung together, staring at the stranger that was looking out at them from the eyes of their dearest friend. If only Angelica and Adverse would turn around! But they did not appear to have noticed that anything was wrong.

Thomas smiled at them. It was not a nice smile. Then he turned back to the window, without another word.

The twins sat as far away from him as they possibly could. Their hearts were hammering, and they felt cold all over. Something terrible had happened to Thomas, they knew that now. *He had been stolen.* The person sitting near them wasn't Thomas at all, but someone – or something – that had stolen Thomas's body and now moved and spoke through it, like a puppet master moves a puppet. That must be why there had been no reflection in the mirror!

So that meant – that meant the real Thomas must be back there – back in the city – helpless, alone . . . lost . . . really lost . . . They must help him! They must! But how could they, with this thing – this thief of Thomas – threatening to turn them to stone? Someone who could do a dangerous and difficult thing like stealing a person's body must be capable of doing just about anything. All Ariel magic was powerful, but this must be the most powerful there was. How could they get Angelica and Adverse's attention without alerting the creature that had stolen Thomas? Pinch and Patch felt quite sure that the Ariel's magic – whoever he was – was more powerful even than Angelica's and Adverse's put together – at least here in Ariel country. Perhaps, as they came down from Ariel lands back into their own country, his powers would grow less and theirs would get stronger. But that would mean the stranger in Thomas's body coming down with them to Owlchurch – there to do who knew what? And it would mean the real Thomas left behind, abandoned in Seraphimia. How long could he last there? The air-sickness would get him, even if nothing else did . . .

Meanwhile, Bird-Thomas rested on the roof of the bakery for a moment, trying to get his breath back. His throat was raw, his eyes stung, he felt dizzy. What had happened, back there? He'd wished that the chimney could open up, and it had. What if he wished again, now?

'I wish,' he whispered, 'I wish I could turn back into myself.'

Nothing happened. His throat didn't swell, no silver smoke came out. And he was still a bird, perched on a roof. Well, maybe that wish had been too hard. But what if he made a smaller wish?

'I wish,' he said, 'I wish I could have a drink of water. My throat's so dry.'

Nothing happened – except that a ray of sun

suddenly lit up a gutter where water dripped, quietly. Thomas flew over to it and drank. His throat began to feel better.

'I wish I could see my friends,' he said, and looked hopefully into the distance. But he saw nothing, except for the sky, and the roof, and the street below. How had that wish worked, the first time? He thought carefully about what had happened, going through each step. Then, quite suddenly, he knew. Those cake crumbs he'd pecked – they'd been from a tray of little iced cakes. He remembered seeing a tray like them before, the first time he'd come into the shop, with Cumulus and the twins. The baker had said they were wish-cakes. And he'd swallowed one of the crumbs! It must have been that that gave him the power for the wish. So perhaps if he got back into the bakery somehow and ate up a whole cake, he'd have a whole lot more wishes . . .

How would he get back into the bakery? He couldn't go back down the chimney. He'd have to try somehow to get back in by the door. He was just about to fly down from the roof when he heard voices below him in the street. One was Signora Anafiela's. The other – the other was a voice he recognised, too. The man who had captured him!

Panic-stricken, Thomas hid behind the chimney pot. He couldn't properly hear what they were saying, only catch a few words. But it was enough to tell him that the kidnapper had already traced him to the bakery, and that the baker was telling him about the bird that had acted so oddly in her shop. There was no way he could go back there now, and he couldn't draw attention to himself by just flying off, either. He'd have to try and hop across the roof to the next one, then the next, and when he was far enough away from them, then fly off. And he'd have to try and follow the dangerous, scary plan he'd thought of before. He'd have to leave Seraphimia and go into the wild sky-paths beyond and . . .

Suddenly, out of the corner of his eye, he saw the kidnapper and the baker look up to the roof. There was no time to lose. He must get away. It was his only chance. I must not get frightened, he thought, wildly. There's nothing else I can do. I have to get away from here, and I must change back into myself and get home.

And so he set off as quietly and stealthily as he could, across the roof, not looking down, hoping that they wouldn't catch his movements. He knew that if the kidnapper caught him again, he'd be lost. There'd be no more chance to get away.

TEN

Metallicus reached the edge of the sky-ocean. Now they were back at the entrance to the shadow-land. The car bumped up on shore and sighed, with unmistakable, deep relief, 'Soon home, soon home,' as it set out on the foggy road through the valley.

Above them, the sun-sailors hovered, unwilling to fly low into the valley. The clouds thickened above the shadow-land so that soon the sun-sailors could not be seen clearly in them, only some reflected light shining weakly down. The air grew close, cold, the shadows drifting thickly around the car, coming right up to the windscreen, the windows. Then the air grew even closer, the cold grew worse, the fog deeper. Metallicus groaned, a deep hollow sound, and shuddered to a stop, then started up again. Now the fog rolled in completely, shrouding the road, the valley, everything.

Adverse cried, 'By the horns of Pan, what's going on, I can't see a thing . . .'

Pinch tried to shout a warning about False Thomas. But as soon as he opened his mouth, the fog filled the car, and settled in instants between the back seat and the front seat, so that they were quite cut off from each other. Then False Thomas turned around to them. They shrank back from him. His eyes had narrowed to slits, the pupils had gone, swallowed up into a burning iris, and his body shone with a strange grey light.

False Thomas hissed, 'True Tom is gone for ever, and I remain.' The voice had changed – it seemed to be coming from far away, and had an odd, hollow ring to it that chilled the very marrow of the twins' bones.

'Not when we're home, you won't,' whispered Pinch, desperately. 'Your magic won't last, in our country. Everyone will know you're not True Tom, but a false thing.'

False Thomas looked at them, and gave a little laugh. 'They will not,' he said, 'for you will not be going back, either.' He waved at the shadows outside. 'You will stay here – and they . . . they will come with me, shaped like you. No one will know the difference.'

'You can't do that,' cried Pinch. 'Adverse! Angelica! Help! Help!'

'They can't hear you,' said False Thomas, and he moved, suddenly, swift as a snake, grabbing their wrists in his hands. His hands were like ice – like fire – and as he held them, they could feel the flesh melting from them, their warm green blood turning to ice in their veins, their skin becoming transparent, their voices catching in their throats like little birds in a trap. They were shrinking, too, becoming smaller, smaller, thinner, till very soon they were as thin and weak as string.

Patch managed to scream, 'Thomas! Thomas! Oh, Thomas, where are you?' before she and Pinch both disappeared, sucked out into the ghastly coldness of the shadow-land like threads pulled through a needle. In the next moment, two formless shapes flowed in through the windows, on to the back seat. False Thomas whispered some words, very low, and breathed on them, and the shadows began to fill out, to thicken, to turn into the shapes of thin, spiky children with Pinch and Patch's faces and tangled hair . . .

Thomas flew on and on. His wings weren't very big, and he was very tired, and his breath was coming harder and harder, so that he couldn't fly very fast. He flew towards the far end of the city – not the quay where they had come in that fateful morning, but the other side. On that side, the lagoon only went for a little way, then petered out into a kind of white marshland which eventually turned into rough, wild country. There were no houses here, and the only paths were small and narrow. There were clumps of cloud-forest everywhere: dark cloud-trees of strange, twisted shapes, which seemed to claw up at Thomas as he flew amongst them. There was a lot of wind here, and he felt very small and very weak, trying to keep going and not be blown away. As he went further and further into the wild country, it began to get darker and darker, the trees to grow closer together, higher and higher. Soon, he could hardly see a thing. Blindly, he kept trying to fly on, not even sure what to look for, not sure what to . . .

Ah! A light, down below! No – two . . . three . . . four . . . five . . . six . . . seven – many lights! They were not still, but moving fast, like headlights racing through the night . . . no, like stars, twinkling, moving rapidly through the sky. Out of breath, cold, scared, he alighted on a low branch of a twisted cloud-tree and looked down. Yes – the lights were definitely moving – very fast – and now . . . now he could see shapes flowing around them – animals – sleek, silver dogs, with red eyes and lights like stars twinkling on their heads – and then . . .

A horse! A gigantic horse, black as night, except for its red, rolling eyes, and the bright star on its brow, and its silver wings, and the bright, moonlight glow of its galloping hooves! And on its back – the biggest, wildest man Thomas had ever seen, in reality or in dream, enormous, bigger even than the Green Man, with a beard reaching down to his waist and a belt of stars around his middle, and a bow and enormous quiver of arrows on his back, and hair of the same darkness as his horse, with silver stars caught in it. And what a face! A face old as time, cruel as the wild, with eyes much darker than night, dark as the time before birth, the time after death. The flying huntsman lifted up a horn to his lips, and blew a single, long, loud note that seemed to ring up and down the wild country, making the trees shiver and shake. And Thomas, too, trapped on his branch, shaking so hard with fear that he actually fell off the branch, and . . .

Directly on to the head of the huntsman's horse! The beast reared and plunged, its hooves striking at the sky, sending sparks of lightning through the air. Thomas narrowly escaped being squashed, and with the last of his strength, tried to make it back to the trees to hide. But the huntsman, yelling aloud, had, fast as light, taken his bow, and loosed an arrow . . . and it sped, fast as thought, straight to Thomas, catching him in the left wing, and pinning him helpless to the trunk of a tree.

The shock nearly took Thomas's breath quite away. He could not move; he was quite numb. He hung, staring, defeated, terrified, while the huntsman calmly dismounted from his horse and came towards him. There was brightness all around Euryon now; his fierce face was all lit up with a shining glow, and all around him his dogs squealed and yelped, little lights around a big one, while his winged horse pawed the ground and snorted and screamed, its red eyes rolling madly.

I'm going to die, thought Thomas. I will never go home. Never. He could feel his life-blood ebbing away, his heart slowing, slowing, moving more and more sluggishly as he began to slip further and further into . . .

The huntsman's huge hand closed over him, and it was suddenly quite dark. Dimly, he felt the arrow being pulled from him. It hurt fiercely. He closed his eyes. Euryon would crush him, and that would be an end to it, all his adventures in the Hidden World come to this terrible end, and on the day of his tenth birthday, too . . .

Pinch and Patch, shadows in the shadow-land, bumped helplessly against each other in the fog. They hung on to each other's hands, but it

was hard even to do that, as shadow-hands do not really know the sense of touch. But they found their voices had come back to them, even if thin and very small, and they kept calling to each other, in fear and grief. They were trapped here now, and False Thomas was travelling with False Pinch and Patch, back to their own country. They would not see their mother again, or their father, or race leaf-boats with Thomas down the River Riddle, or eat Cumulus's cakes or play glamouring tricks . . . All their earthly magic had left them and all they could do was drift on and on, carried further and further into the foggy valley of the shadow-land. They had never been so afraid, and never felt so helpless. They were children of the Hidden World, and not used to feeling like this. Who could help them now? This was a place worse even than Pandemonium, the city of the Uncouthers – and if they could not get out of here, and soon, too, they knew they would become shadows for ever, and in time lose even their voices . . . Their spirits would float trapped between lands, and never, never would they . . .

Patch shook herself. No! She would not give up! 'Pinch,' she said, trying to sound brave, 'we have to get out of here, straight away.'

'That's all very well,' whispered Pinch, 'but how?'

'We can ride the breeze, drift with the air,' said Patch.

'That's what we're doing now, drifting,' said Pinch. 'We're getting nowhere, just round and round in circles...'

'We can try and steer,' said Patch. 'Think of the long-stalking spell.' 'Long-stalking' was covering great distances in one step – it turned ordinary shoes into seven-league boots.

'Our shoes are shadows too,' said Pinch. 'It won't work. Anyway, in this fog – how do we know which way to go?'

'I don't know,' said Patch, 'I only know we can't just stay here and wait to just melt away like snow in the sun and never return home. And I think we do not try to go home, for that would take too long and False Thomas will be there before us. We must try and get back to Seraphimia. We must find Thomas, our real Thomas, our True Tom. We have to save him, or we won't save ourselves either.'

'OK,' said Pinch, 'but if we don't know which way to go . . .'

'Are you ready to try?' cried Patch.

'Yes,' said Pinch, quietly, 'I am.'

So they linked shadow-arms and they said, very loudly, the long-stalking spell. It didn't work. They tried again. Still nothing. In desperation, Pinch called out, 'Oh powers of the shadow-land, help us! A wicked Ariel has taken two of your creatures, and we must defeat him. Oh, please, powers of the shadow-lands, help us get back to Seraphimia and defeat him!'

Suddenly, a gust of wind-shadow shaped vaguely like a misty horse raced up the valley towards them. In the next instant, the fog parted, for a moment, like a curtain opening, and they could see the sky-ocean shimmering only a short distance away. It was only for an instant, but it was enough. The shadow-twins jumped up on to the back of the wind-horse, and holding on to its misty mane, called, 'To Seraphimia, go, fast!'

Warmth was creeping back into Thomas, though he still felt numb. Was this death? he thought. He'd always imagined it was a cold, cold feeling. But he was warming up. Definitely. And the wound in his wing throbbed horribly. His heart beat fast. He was still enclosed in the darkness of the huntsman's hand. If he wasn't dead – what was Euryon going to do with him? Why hadn't the flying huntsman simply squashed him?

Light fell in on him, and he blinked, frightened. Euryon had opened his hand, and was lifting it slowly to his face. He's going to eat me! thought Thomas, terrified. He opened his beak and gave a despairing twitter, trying to scream, 'No, please! Please! Don't eat me! I don't belong here! I'm a human, I'm a Rymer!'

Then there came a deep, rumbling voice, a voice that spoke words in a language Thomas didn't know, but that, strangely, he found he could understand. It said, 'A human? Up here, in the wild sky-country? Never! Little bird, you lie!'

He can understand me, thought Thomas, amazed, forgetting for a moment that the star-giant was from the beginning of time, the morning of the world, and thus not bound by Ariel magic. 'I do not lie, sir,' he twittered, wildly, 'please listen, sir – a wicked Ariel has turned me into this shape but I'm a Rymer, it is true, and my name is Thomas Trew!'

The giant gave a big, big laugh. 'True Thomas! You have returned! I met you last time you came, do you not remember?'

'I do not think it was me, sir, for I was never

here before,' said Thomas, faintly.

'Well, then, someone like you. You humans have such short lives, gone like a puff of wind. What do you do here, little Rymer? Do you not know it is dangerous, when Euryon rides on the hunt? Are you not afraid?'

'I . . . I have come to meet you, sir,' faltered Thomas. 'To . . . to give you a gift.' Am I mad, he thought to himself. What gift? I have nothing to give him, nothing at all!

'To meet me? To give me a gift!' The storm-giant lifted up his head and roared with laughter. The laughter was like thunder rumbling through the sky. 'You are the first such! Mostly, they flee before me, for I break their necks like twigs and crunch their bones and swallow their spirits like draughts of wine!' He picked Thomas up by the wounded wing and dangled him from one giant finger, laughing. 'You are a small mouthful, Rymer bird, True Tom or whatever you are, but your spirit might be refreshing indeed, for you are not afraid!'

He tilted his head up and Thomas saw right into his enormous, cavernous mouth, with its rows of shining, huge, needle-sharp teeth. His wing hurt dreadfully, and he knew his last hour had come, for it was pointless trying to argue with an outlaw force of nature like Euryon, or appealing to his mercy. His heart nearly gave way then, but at that very moment, he heard something he had not heard for a very long time, not since the time he had been in despair and darkness in the grim city of Pandemonium. He heard the sound of a flute. He knew the tune. It was one of his mother's songs! It was the sound of her flute!

It gave him just the last bit of courage that he needed. Twisting himself free of Euryon's grip – the fierce pain from his wing impossible to describe – he fell through the air, whirling down and down, and as he went, suddenly, his mother's song poured from his bird's throat, to the tune of the flute. As he sang, he felt his strength returning, and as the notes of the flute died away, his song rose, stronger and stronger, higher and higher, and so did he, rising up into the air on the wings of song. He sang of the earth, and of Owlchurch, and of his father waiting for him, and his friends – and of sailing leaf-boats down the river, and of all the countries he had visited since he had come in the Hidden World, and his adventures, and his longing to be back on the earth, safe and sound. He sang and sang and hardly noticed that Euryon stood stock-still, with his restless dogs still too, and his red-eyed horse. Yet the stars on their brows seemed to dance, to sway, in time to Thomas's song.

At last, the song died away. Dizzy, Thomas hovered an instant, then plunged like an arrow to the ground. But he never reached it, for a hand had shot out, and held him – gently, this time. Through the throbbing pain of his wing, Thomas heard the rumbling voice saying, very softly, 'I have not heard such a thing since the beginning of time, the morning of the world. Is that the gift you came to give me, Rymer?'

Thomas did not answer. He found he could not. His throat was thick and hot and hurt a lot.

The huntsman did not seem to notice. He said, 'It is a good gift. No one has given me such a thing, in a very long time. So now. You have given me this gift, and I will let you go safe.'

'Please,' said Thomas, finding his voice again. 'Please – will you do one thing for me in return?'

The storm-giant's laugh boomed loudly through the sky. 'You are brave for such a small thing! But a gift calls for a gift in return. What do you want? A star from the sky, to hang in your window? The power to crush men's skulls like fruit? The gift of blazing lightning, to ravage and burn?'

'Oh, no, thank you,' said Thomas, eagerly. 'I would like my own shape. I am not a bird. I am a boy. A human boy. The magic that changed my shape – could you break it, sir?'

'Is that all?' said the giant, and swooping down, he picked Thomas up, delicately, between thumb and forefinger. With the other hand, he plucked a star from his tangled hair. He blew on it, carefully. A shower of silver dust came from it. The giant sprinkled the stardust on Thomas. He said, 'As the stars return to the sky, return to what you should be.'

A hot pain shot through Thomas. He screamed as his wounded wing suddenly sprang out, stiffly, then stretched, changed, and became an arm. Then the other – then his face, his body, his legs. In the blink of an eye, he was back to his own shape. But his left arm hung, helpless, hurting almost more than Thomas could bear. He said, in a very faint voice, 'Thank you . . . thank you . . . I . . .' and then he fainted, clean away.

ELEVEN

On the back of the wind-horse, Pinch and Patch drifted fast out of the mouth of the valley of shadows, and out into the brightness of the sky-ocean shore. Faster, faster went the wind-horse, and faster still, till in a twinkling they were hovering over the domes of Seraphimia. Then the wind-horse reared, and bucked, and threw them off. They fell tumbling through the air to the pavements of the city, but because their bodies were now so thin and shadowy, no one saw them land, and they did not hurt themselves at all.

'Right,' said Patch, as they landed, 'we must go and get help at once. We've got to get our

proper shapes back first, before it's too late.'

'Who do you think can help?'

'That funny old witch, I think,' said Patch. 'Hecate Longnose. She seemed nice.'

'But it might have been her who did this,' pointed out Pinch.

'No way,' said Patch, firmly. 'It was Astrolir.'

'The star-reader? But why?'

'I don't know. But I'm sure it was him. I was thinking about it while we were flying here. You saw the way he was with False Thomas. He was . . . he was sort of coaching him to speak!'

'You're right!' cried Pinch. 'For once in your life,' he added, hurriedly, in case Patch might get a swollen head . . .

They raced through the streets towards Hecate Longnose's house. Even for a Hidden Worlder, being thinned carries risks that are greatly increased as time goes on. If you're thinned too long, you can get stuck in the weird nowhere place where only shadows and ghosts may safely exist. And if the thinning has been done not by your own free will, but by someone else's spell, it's even more dangerous.

Reaching the witch's house, they flowed in through her keyhole – at least this shape had some advantage! – and through the rooms of the house, looking for Hecate. At last, they found her in the attic, sorting out bunches of dried herbs into little sachets. They flowed around her, calling her name. Now, if Astrolir had had time to make the same strong kind of spell against them that he'd made against Thomas, the twins would have had a good deal of trouble even making Hecate realise they were there. But he'd not had time, the spell was much weaker, and so Hecate heard their voices. Far away, they sounded, and thin, and buzzing, but the old witch could recognise the voices, as being those of the rude young things who'd come knocking at her door earlier and left in such a tearing hurry.

'Well, I never!' she said, crossly. 'You've come back! What's up this time? And where's your friend? You'd better be going, all of you – the alarms have rung, for Euryon is on his way to the city!'

She cupped a hand to her ear as the twins buzzed excitedly around her, trying to tell her everything all at once. She held up a hand. 'One at a time, one at a time! And slowly!'

It was agonising for the twins, being kept in thinning while the old witch calmly made them go through their story, very carefully. But they managed it; and when they'd finished, Hecate's comfortable old face looked very grim indeed. 'By the Moon!' she exclaimed. 'It is hard to believe one of ours could be so wicked . . . but Astrolir has looked on the star-paths for too long and maybe it has sent him mad. I cannot understand why he would have done this, but it is a serious business, a very serious business indeed. Now then, children, let's get you smartly back into your own shape, and go and pay a visit on Astrolir!'

* * *

When Thomas came to, he found he was perched on the huntsman's horse, just in front of the storm-giant himself. They were galloping fast through the wild country, the dogs streaking beside them like silver shadows. Thomas's eyes and mouth were full of rushing wind, and there was the beat of blood in his ears, and the beat of pain in his arm, which hung uselessly by his side. He dared to look up – and caught a glimpse of the huntsman's fierce face, the hair streaming behind him like the horse's mane, and heard the storm-giant's sudden shout of wild joy as they rode faster, faster, at more and more breakneck speed.

He whispered, 'Where are we going, sir?'

'To Seraphimia, of course,' came the huntsman's rumbling voice.

'That is kind of you, sir. Thank you so much. I do not know how I would have got there if . . .'

'Pah! Don't thank me. I wager they will pay a good deal for the safe return of a Rymer, is that not so?'

Thomas gulped. '*Pay*, sir?'

'Yes, pay! I said I would let you go safe, and I will,' rumbled the storm-giant. 'But you cannot expect me to hold such a valuable thing and simply let it go unpaid. Your song was a great gift, but you are an honoured guest of the Ariels and it is their fault you are in this state. It is only fair that they pay me. Besides, I am a hunter, a raider, an outlaw, and Seraphimia is fat and rich. I take you to the Ariels – but they must pay to have you back. And pay well. Better than they've ever paid before!'

Thomas nodded, helplessly. There was nothing he could say.

'Ariel gold's the thing,' said Euryon. 'Rivers of Ariel gold – and maybe more.' Suddenly, he drew up his horse. It pawed and snorted, and blew through its nose, while the dogs milled around its feet, lifting up their heads and howling, silently, their slitted red eyes fixed upwards on Thomas, watching his every movement. 'Look,' said the huntsman, pointing with his whip to the west. 'The sun is sinking, the domes of the city shine – and my time has come!'

He dug his heels into the horse's flanks and they were off again, faster than the wind, faster than light, faster than thought. And in less time than it takes to say it, they were outside the great city of Seraphimia, which glowed with the last bit of the sunlight. There was a tall watchtower at this end of the city, looking over the marshlands beyond the lagoon. As soon as they came near, Thomas heard alarm bells ringing, louder and louder, voices shouting, shutters and doors slamming, as the whole city shut down at the arrival of the star-giant.

But Euryon stood up in his stirrups and shouted, 'Euryon! Euryon of the Stormy Stars challenges Seraphimia, City of the Heavens! Send out an envoy, for I have been on the hunt, and have a prize worth the buying!'

Hecate Longnose and the twins, now restored to their own shapes, hurried through the city to the star-reader's house. But there was no answer to their knock on the door, though they banged on it again and again. Hecate Longnose tried a spell to force the door open, but it wouldn't budge. They were just about to give up and go away when all at once, Patch yelled, very loudly. Both the others jumped.

'What's the matter?' cried Pinch.

'Something nipped my toe – ow – ow!' yelled Patch, hopping up and down. 'Oh – it's a rat! A rat!' They looked where she was pointing and saw a small, bright-eyed rat sitting on the doorstep of the house, calmly grooming its whiskers. Patch cried, 'You rotten little thing!' and took off her shoe ready to throw it at the rat. But it did not budge. It sat up on its haunches and stared at them and squeaked, once, twice, three times.

'Wait – this is no ordinary creature,' said the old witch, staring at the rat. 'This is a metamorph. Someone's been monkeying with some bad magic . . .'

The rat nodded his head, vigorously.

'You can't talk to us, is that right?' said Hecate.

The rat nodded.

'Is it Astrolir who did this to you?' The rat looked puzzled. 'The star-reader – who lives here – tall, thin chap – spectacles . . .'

The rat nodded so hard his head seemed in danger of falling off.

'Are you Thomas Trew?'

The rat shook its head, slowly.

'Then where is he?'

The rat stuck its front legs at either side of it, in the shape of wings.

'He's flown away?' said Hecate.

The rat nodded.

'Then he's a metamorph too? A bird?'

The rat nodded, hard.

'Did Astrolir make him fly away?'

The rat shook his head, firmly. He pointed to himself, then made the wing shape again.

'You and Thomas did it?'

Yes, nodded the rat.

'Where is Thomas now?'

The rat shrugged.

'Who are you?' cried Pinch, unable to keep quiet any longer. The rat stared at him with bright eyes. Then he made a rapid gesture – the shape of a circle, but with little circles inside it, like a whirling ball of string, unravelling. Both Hecate and the twins knew what that symbol meant.

'You're a Trickster!' exclaimed Patch. 'Are you an Ariel?'

The rat shook his head. He pointed down.

'You're from earth,' said Pinch. 'You're one of us – you're a Middler!'

The rat nodded, baring his sharp teeth in a smile.

'How did you get into such a pickle, if you're a Trickster?' said Hecate, suspiciously.

The rat shrugged and looked embarrassed. Then he put his head to one side and laid it on one paw, and closed his eyes.

'You were asleep?'

The rat's eyes flew open. He nodded, sheepishly.

'Do you know where Astrolir is?' said Hecate.

The rat pointed down the street. He sniffed at the ground. He pointed. Again, he made the shape of wings, and then shaded his eyes, looking.

'He's gone looking for Thomas?'

The rat nodded. He pointed at himself, then at Hecate. He fixed his eyes pleadingly on her.

'You will help us sniff him out, if I break the spell on you? Very well. But it will take time – quite a bit of time. It smells like a very strong spell he's put on you – not a hurried one like he put on the twins. You—'

'Please, Miss Longnose,' broke in Patch, 'please, I don't think we have much time.' She crouched down near the rat. 'Please – will you take us first to where the star-reader is? We've got to make sure he can't catch Thomas again . . . we've got to make him tell us exactly what he did to Thomas . . . Please – Thomas

148

may die if he stays here too long and not in his own shape – please . . . He's a human, not a Hidden Worlder, and they're much frailer than we are.'

The rat stared at her, then at Hecate.

'It would be best,' said the old witch. 'On my word I promise I'll help you, Mr Rat, as soon as this is finished. Will you please take us now?'

The rat nodded, slowly. Then all at once, he ran straight at Patch, and before she had time to do more than squeak, the rat had run up her leg, up her body, and on to her shoulder, where he sat preening himself.

Pinch laughed. 'You do look funny!' he said.

At that moment, all the bells in the city began to ring, deafeningly loud. Hecate Longnose shouted above the hubbub, 'The flying huntsman is approaching! Let's hope your Thomas isn't anywhere near him or nothing we can do can save him! Now, Rat, guide us very quickly to where you think Astrolir was headed.'

* * *

Outside the city, Euryon repeated his challenge, once, twice, three times. At the third time, the air was suddenly full of the buzzing of sun-sailors, flying in formation towards them. Euryon shouted, 'Duke of Seraphimia! Bring your soldiers one step closer to me and I will fry them out of the sky! I come to offer you a bargain, not a fight!'

The sun-sailors retreated. A window opened in the watchtower. Someone appeared at the window – a very tall golden-skinned Ariel, in pure black armour.

'Take care!' shouted Euryon. 'I said no soldiers!'

The soldier stepped aside, revealing someone else, a tall thin man in plain robes, whose spectacles glinted in the setting sun.

Thomas gave a little cry. 'It's him!'

Euryon growled, 'Who?'

'The Ariel who turned me into a bird and took my shadow from me and sent it in my place . . .'

'Ah,' said Euryon. 'That is odd.'

'Why?'

But Euryon didn't answer Thomas's question. Instead, he picked him up, bodily, and holding him up, shouted at the watchtower window, 'Augustus Astrolir of the Astrolir clan, you whose people follow the tracks of all my people, why are you here?'

The star-reader looked startled for an instant. Then his voice floated down to them. It sounded a little anxious. 'You have the Rymer, Euryon.'

'That is so,' growled the star-giant.

'His spirit is strong,' said the star-reader. 'Devouring it will sustain you for many a long year.'

'Is that so?' The huntsman's hands tightened on Thomas, making him cry out in pain.

'Oh, yes, my lord. If you devour him, you will not feel hungry again for a long while. You can enjoy being in your own lands and . . .'

Euryon dropped Thomas back into the

saddle. He stood up in his stirrups. His voice was full of contempt as he shouted, 'You mean, I can leave you alone? Is that it? Is that why you took this boy and metamorphed him? You think you can buy my obedience, and your peace, with the living gift of a Rymer? Then you are a bigger fool than I thought. I catch and kill my own, Astrolir. Never forget that. Besides, I have given my word. The boy is safe. He gave me a gift. You are too late, Astrolir.'

'But, my lord . . .'

'Go away. I have not come to speak with you, but to barter for this boy's life with the Duke, not a no-account like you.'

'Then you will be disappointed,' shouted Astrolir. His tone had changed completely. 'We do not care what happens to him. I have spoken to the Duke. He agrees with me.'

'Does he agree with what you did?'

'Well, he did not know I would do it, but he approves, now. For we know something you should know too – something I discovered in my star-books only the other day. If you have the Rymer, your way here is barred for five centuries. We have no use for him, and his friends have no use for him. No one has come to find him. No one cares. Keep him, eat him, make him your slave or your pet, just as you like. We don't care.'

'I want to speak to the Duke,' yelled Euryon.

'Very well,' said Astrolir, and stepped aside to let the Duke approach the window. With his halo of golden hair, he stood there, looking mildly annoyed.

'I am here, Euryon. Why are you making so much noise?'

'I have the Rymer,' said the flying huntsman, but there was a new uncertainty in his voice. 'He is valuable. He must be worth . . .'

'Strictly nothing,' said the Duke, crossly. 'Do what you like with him.'

'But . . . is that the word of Count Cirrus too? Of the Council of Seraphimia? Of the guilds? Of everyone in the city?'

'It does not matter,' snapped the Duke. 'I'm in charge here. The others have to do as I say.'

'He was your guest,' said Euryon, grimly. 'He was under your protection. How can Seraphimia have fallen so low as to betray a guest?'

'How dare a savage like you give us lectures?' cried Astrolir. 'Enough's enough, Euryon. I make you a gift of the Rymer, and with that I bind you back into your own lands. For five centuries, you will not be able to cross even the marshes. You will have to leave us in peace.'

As he spoke, the huntsman's horse began to back up, slowly, as if pushed by an irresistible force. Back, back, they were being pushed through the marshlands, back into the wild country, with the huntsman yelling bloodcurdling cries, and the dogs howling silently, and the horse puffing, snorting, whinnying, and the bells of the city ringing deafeningly over the lagoon and the marshes. Thomas could feel his heart sinking and his breath coming cold and sharp and his arm hurting like fire, and he knew then that it was all too late, and that Astrolir had won.

Then the huntsman halted. He threw back his head, and yelled so loudly that the whole air rang with his fierce words. 'People of Seraphimia! Your own leader has betrayed your guest, the Rymer, and delivered him into my hands! You might keep me out, but you will not keep out the rest of the Hidden World! People of Seraphimia! Are you willing to be traitors and outcasts for ever?'

Pinch and Patch and Hecate ran through the panic-stricken city. People ran hither and thither, shouting that the flying huntsman was on his way and that he was bearing down very fast, and seemed in the most savage of moods. They followed the directions of the little rat as he pointed them this way and that way. Soon Hecate exclaimed, 'We're going down to the furthest defences, to the watchtower at the edge of the lagoon! What is Astrolir doing?

Surely he does not think Thomas is out there?'

Pinch and Patch did not bother replying, for they had no idea. But instinct made them know that something really bad was happening, and that Thomas was in the gravest danger he'd ever been in since the time he'd almost been flung into Deepfire by the Uncouthers.

Finally, they reached the city wall, and came to the watchtower. It loomed tall and straight and grey and forbidding, quite unlike most of the other buildings in Seraphimia. There were sentries in black armour at the door down the bottom, but Hecate made a couple of rapid gestures over them, and they froze as if turned to statues. They pushed past them, through the open doorway, and up the stairs. There were a lot of them, going up up up in a corkscrew pattern. On Patch's shoulder, Rat was hopping up and down with excitement – a rather painful experience for Patch. Faster, he seemed to be saying, faster, it's him, it's him, and he's up to no good!

At last, they reached a landing. There were more black-armoured sentries there. They stared, surprised; and kept on staring, for in an instant Hecate had frozen them, too. Past the sentries, and up some more stairs, even more narrow than before; and finally, bursting into a large, dusty room up at the top. And there, turning towards them with surprised yelps – Astrolir, and Duke Nimbus!

'Hecate! What are you doing here!' shouted Astrolir, at the same moment as the Duke snapped, 'What is the meaning of this, Signora Longnose!'

Then Astrolir saw the twins. He screamed, 'How did you get here! You were meant to be . . .'

'Stuck in the shadow-land, yes,' said Pinch.

'But we got out, see,' said Patch.

'Not for long,' said Astrolir, smiling nastily, and raised an arm. But Hecate had raised hers too, and the spells met each other head on, and shattered, sending showers of ghastly, earsplitting sound spinning around the room.

'Will you stop that!' shouted the Duke, as Astrolir raised an arm again. 'It gives me a headache!' He pointed a finger at the twins. 'Why are you here again? We farewelled you not long ago, with your friend . . .'

'It wasn't our friend, sir! It was a false thing, a copy! This magician snatched our friend and transformed him, and—'

'Oh, I don't want to know the details,' snapped the Duke. 'I may not approve of all his methods, but Astrolir has done the right thing. He has saved our city from the depredations of the flying huntsman for a long time to come. So it is a small price to pay, giving the Rymer to Euryon. What good are humans to us, anyway?'

Hecate went pale. She stared at him. She began, 'Your Grace, surely you have not really . . .'

But Pinch and Patch, with howls of rage, had flung themselves at the Duke. Surprised, he stumbled, tripped and fell. They fell on top of him, punching him, kicking him, slapping him, scratching him. The rat jumped off Patch's shoulder and joined in, nipping at his toes. Meanwhile, Hecate, recovering, had launched herself at Astrolir – or rather, launched a flurry of horrid little spells like a cloud of biting fleas or midges, which flew into the star-reader's nose, and eyes and ears and mouth. Yelping, choking, he tried to brush them off, to say spells of his own, but the spell-midges kept coming. 'Mercy! Mercy! Stop! Stop!' he croaked.

'Not till you turn this rat back to his own shape, and tell us exactly where Thomas is,' hissed Hecate.

The twins, meanwhile, were sitting on top of the Duke, glaring at him, their eyes glowing with a fierce green light. Despite his size, the Duke seemed frightened, cowering on the floor as if he were half their size, and screeching every time the rat took a good bite on his flesh.

Pinch growled, 'Have you really given

Thomas to the huntsman?'

'If you have, all the Hidden World will go to war against the Ariels,' hissed Patch.

'And we will kill you,' said Pinch.

'And the rat bite you to death,' said Patch.

'Tell us!' said Pinch, menacingly.

'Well – no – yes – you see . . . It can't be stopped now – Astrolir's star-books – it said . . . It's all his fault!' wailed the Duke. 'I shouldn't have listened to him, but I did. I think he put a spell on me . . . I think he . . .'

At that moment, steps sounded outside, and a crowd of people came bursting in. At their head was Count Cirrus, with soldiers behind him.

'Your Grace, I heard a terrible rumour . . .' he began, then stopped. Before he could order the soldiers to do anything, Pinch and Patch jumped off the Duke and ran towards him, crying, 'They gave Thomas to the huntsman! They betrayed our friend! They are worse than the Uncouthers!'

'That's what I heard,' said Cirrus, slowly. 'They say the flying huntsman is shouting it over the rooftops and in the air! But surely . . . surely – I just can't believe it . . . I . . .'

No, Cirrus, no!' shouted the Duke. 'It was all Astrolir's idea . . . he . . . I think he er . . . put me under a spell . . . Cirrus, I want you to arrest him at once . . . Cirrus, quick, quick, he's getting away!'

Too late! For Astrolir, seeing he was abandoned by the Duke, managed to knock over Hecate, with a desperate lunge. He made the rapid gesture she'd made before, and instantly everyone was frozen to the spot for a moment, long enough for Astrolir to dodge past and run away down the stairs as fast as his legs could carry him.

TWELVE

The rat was the first to recover. Without waiting for the Duke's shout of 'After him!' he dashed down the stairs after the star-reader, with the Gull twins in close pursuit. But Astrolir had reached the bottom and escaped out of the tower before they had reached the landing. By the time they had burst out into the street, they were only just in time to see a sun-sailor rising high up into the air – with Astrolir clearly visible at the controls!

'Drat!' said the rat. 'He'll get away, now. He knows all the star-paths and he can hide anywhere in the sky. They'll never get him. Drat. I'll have to stay for ever a rat.'

The twins stared at him. 'You spoke,' said Pinch, slowly.

'Of course I—' began the rat, crossly, then catching himself up, he shouted, 'Yahoo! If you can understand me, the spell must be lifting anyway!'

'That was my doing,' said Hecate, appearing on the scene at that moment, 'and the fact that Astrolir's run away, so the spell is weakening.'

The rat's legs were getting longer, his face broader, his chest thicker, his whiskers longer. In the flicker of an instant, he had turned into a little man, shorter than a dwarf, wearing a long beard and shabby velvet trousers and jacket of the same colour as the rat's fur. His tail was gone, but his bare chest was rather hairy, as were his bare feet, and his eyes were bright as the rat's had been.

He gave a broad grin, showing a row of sharp white teeth, exactly like the rat's. He bowed. 'Ratshaun O'Rattus at your service,' he said. 'Ratty for short. I'm a leprechaun.'

'We can see that,' said Patch. 'OK, Ratty, if you're a leprechaun, then you'll have a few tricks up your sleeves. Forget Astrolir. We need to rescue Thomas.'

At that moment, Count Cirrus, with the soldiers after him, came panting out into the street. 'Where's Astrolir?' he shouted.

The leprechaun pointed up. 'Hijacked one of your sun-sailors and took off into the wild blue yonder, towards the rising sun. Seen the last of him, I should say.'

'We certainly haven't,' said the Count, grimly. 'He's got to stand trial for his treachery.' He motioned to the soldiers. 'You, you, and you! Get that sun-sailor over there and get after him. Don't bother coming back till you've got him.' The soldiers set off at a run. Instants later, the craft rose into the air and swiftly vanished to the east.

'What about Thomas?' cried Patch.

'You should have sent your soldiers after Euryon, first,' said Pinch.

Count Cirrus looked sad. 'I'm sorry. It's too late for the Rymer. Astrolir bound him into Euryon's grasp. He cannot escape from it, or be rescued from it.'

'Rubbish!' yelled Patch. 'You've got to try! You've got to, or else the Middlers will declare war on all of you, no matter what! Yes, and the Montaynards too, and the Seafolk, and . . . and . . .' She burst into angry tears.

Count Cirrus looked very uncomfortable. 'Believe me, Miss Gull, I wish I could help. But we can't take back Astrolir's words.'

'That can't be right!' shouted Pinch. 'What about how the spell lifted on Ratty?'

Hecate broke in. 'I'm sorry, children, but Count Cirrus is right. The words are binding. Short of the flying huntsman willingly giving up his prey, there's very little we can do.'

'And the flying huntsman never gives up his prey,' said Count Cirrus, gloomily.

Just then, the Duke, looking rather the worse for wear, stumbled out of the watchtower. With a cry of rage, the twins threw themselves on him.

'You rotten, horrid, rotten, rotten man!' screeched Patch.

'You murderer, you traitor!' yelled Pinch.

'Get them off me!' roared the Duke. 'Cirrus, get these children off me at once!'

'Not till you get our friend back!' cried Patch.

'Not till you make the flying huntsman give him back!' added Pinch.

'I can't, you fool! I can't! Did you hear me, Cirrus! Get these children off me! That's an order from your Duke!'

'There is no Duke,' said Cirrus, with a tight, hard smile. 'The position is vacant. And I don't take orders from a civilian.' With that, he motioned to his soldiers. 'Come. There is work to be done, if we are to choose a new Duke.'

'Cirrus!' roared Duke Nimbus. 'This is treachery! This is mutiny! I command you to—'

'You command nothing,' said Cirrus, coldly.

'You are to appear before a Council meeting. It will decide your fate.'

'How dare you!' shouted the Duke, and throwing off the children, he made a lunge at Cirrus. But the soldiers stopped him, and holding him by both arms, they marched away down the street, in the direction of the palace.

'I'm sorry,' said Cirrus again, as he turned to follow them. 'I really wish there was something I could do right now.'

'Let us at least take a sun-sailor and go looking for him, sir,' said Ratty.

Cirrus shook his head. 'Sorry. Can't be done. The sun-sailors can't go through that wild country. It confuses their navigation systems and they crash. But we will escort you back home to Middler country, you, and the twins, and try and sort out this terrible situation. Rest assured we will punish Astrolir and Nimbus.'

'What's the good of that to us, if our friend is lost to us for ever?' wept Patch.

'Perhaps,' said Hecate, gently, 'perhaps, in

time, with the help of the other Hidden Worlders, we can try and force Euryon to give up the Rymer . . .'

'We want to do that now,' snapped Pinch. 'Now, do you hear! He can't last, out there!'

'No, it is really—' began Hecate, when, suddenly, Ratty interrupted her.

'I've got an idea!' he said.

Thomas sat slumped in Euryon's saddle as the horse made his way slowly back into the wild cloud-country. He felt numb. Beyond tears, beyond fear, beyond anything at all. He was lost to his home, his father, his friends, his life. How long would he last? How long would Euryon's patience last? Who knew what the flying huntsman might do next? Maybe he'd take it into his head to play a cruel game with him, or to dangle him over space, or even to eat him . . .

Even these dark thoughts hardly made more than a tiny ripple of fear pass through him. He wasn't really scared of the flying huntsman any more. The terrible pain in his arm hardly bothered him at all, either. He could feel his mind and his spirit slowly slipping away. Then he looked down at himself and saw with an odd little start that his skin was becoming transparent. His very body was vanishing . . . slipping into the nowhere place, the world behind even the Hidden World . . . going step by helpless step into that strange place where ghosts wander and shadows lurk . . .

It was very, very quiet. Euryon did not speak to him. The dogs were silent, the horse himself made not a sound as he picked his way delicately through the trackless waste. There was no breath of wind, no air. The cloud-country looked more and more grim and forbidding the more they went into it. The clouds were piled up in big thunderous masses now, and no light from the sun or the moon struck through.

Thomas began to feel cold. So cold. It was as

though he'd never get warm again . . . never . . . ever . . . With the last of his strength, he tried to summon up his mother's song, the song that had saved him from the huntsman, the song full of light, and life, and love. But he couldn't hear it any more. He couldn't remember it. He was too cold. His brain had seized up, and his spirit was sluggish. Soon, he would stop caring at all. His eyes closed. His whole being began to fog up, to slip away, to vanish . . .

'Do you really think it will work?' said Patch, anxiously.

'Let's hope so,' shrugged Ratty. Leaning over the controls, he peered through the windscreen. 'We'll know soon enough. Here's the first of the cloud-country. Nasty-looking stuff. Cloud's almost green – big, big storm coming, I'd say. Brace yourselves, chaps.' He crooned, almost under his breath, 'Cloud-sailor, dear friend, cloud-sailor, take us through unharmed . . .'

As he finished saying the last few words, there was a tremendous jolt. Pinch and Patch and Hecate shouted out loud.

'Never mind, chaps,' said Ratty, grinning broadly. 'Just a bit of a bump there. But we're in!'

Cloud rushed past them, angry-looking cloud, swirling in boiling formations all around them. Pinch faltered, 'Hope we're not going to crash . . .'

'Don't say that, don't say that,' said Ratty, sharply. 'Our dear friend the cloud-sailor will see us through. This is her own home, she knows it so well . . .'

Underneath their feet the craft hummed and hiccuped, then settled into a low purr. Ratty said, 'She agrees, see . . . Hey! What a sweet baby this craft is!' He looked very pleased with himself, as well he might – he had tricked the sun-sailor into thinking it was a cloud-sailor.

'Now we're in,' said Hecate, 'let's find the path of the huntsman . . .' She opened out a folded map on her lap. In one corner was a little label: 'Property of Augustus Astrolir, Chief Star-Reader of Seraphimia'. 'Astrolir tracked Euryon on this path,' she said, jabbing at a bright line on the map. 'He's likely to be headed back this way . . . These are the directions you need to give the sun – er – the cloud-sailor, Ratty. That way, down through this bank of cloud, and down past that cloud-range, into this valley – there should be a break here, we should be able to see a little more . . .'

'Aye, aye, ma'am!' said Ratty, jauntily, and turned the wheel in the right direction, crooning, 'Dear cloud-sailor, dear friend, we find the path of the storm-giant of ancient fame . . .'

Another big jolt, and a sudden rush down, like going down very quickly in a lift. The twins and Hecate shouted. But very soon the craft righted itself and began humming onwards.

Now the cloud was less thick and they could

see vaguely down through it.

'It looks so wild and lonely,' said Patch, her nose pressed up against the porthole of the ship.

'That's because it is,' whispered Hecate. 'This is outlaw territory.'

Suddenly, Pinch gave a shout. 'I can see something! I can see something! Something running – lots of things – dogs! Dogs! They're dogs! And a horse – the biggest horse I ever saw – and a man, oh Pan strike us! Look at the size of him!'

'Thomas, Thomas, where's Thomas?' shouted Patch, pushing up beside him. 'I can't see him . . . Where is he? Oh, where is he?'

Hecate and Ratty looked at each other. In their minds was the same thought. Perhaps Euryon had indeed devoured Thomas. Or maybe simply dumped him somewhere . . .

'No, no, I see him!' said Pinch. 'There – oh, quick, quick, he looks . . . he looks . . .'

'No, he's not dead,' screamed Patch. 'He can't

be! He's our friend! We love him! We've got to take him home!' She fought with the catch on the porthole, trying to open it, while Ratty and Hecate yelled at her to stop it, and Pinch shouted, 'We've got to get him! We've got to, don't you see!'

Down below, Euryon suddenly drew up his horse. So sudden was it that the dogs kept running for quite a while before realising their master had stopped. The flying huntsman stood up in his stirrups and shook his huge fist at the craft buzzing above him.

'You intrude, Ariels!' he roared. 'You intrude into country that is not yours! You will not force me to do anything! I will call down all the storms to crush and destroy you!'

In the saddle, Thomas slumped, still, hardly even breathing at all.

'He's shouting something at us!' said Pinch.

'Probably that he's going to call up storms

and kill us,' said Hecate. She was very pale. 'He can do it, too. No sun-sailor has ever— I mean,' she hurried on, as the craft lurched sickeningly downwards, 'I mean, this is a beautiful cloud-sailor but she . . .'

But Patch, still wrestling with the porthole, finally got it open. Streams of freezing air rushed in, and torn rags of cloud. Before anyone could stop Patch, she had half leaned out of the window and bellowed down to Euryon, 'Please, dear sir, please, my lord, we do not want to harm you. We are not Ariels, but Middlers, and we only want our friend Thomas back . . .'

'Yes,' said Pinch, shouting down in his turn, 'please, let him go, this is not Thomas's place, and he's going to die!'

'What's that you say?' shouted Euryon. 'Meddlers, are you? I'll say so.' Suddenly, he seemed to grow taller and taller and taller, stretching out like a massive thundercloud, his face purpling with rage. 'Get out of my country, or I'll kill you all!'

'Thomas! Thomas! Please, we only want Thomas!' said Patch, before Hecate rushed over to her, pulled her and Pinch down from the porthole, shut it, and barred the way.

'Are you crazy?' said the old witch.

'Stand aside!' shouted the twins, struggling to get back to the porthole.

Thomas stirred in the saddle. Dimly, in the fast-sinking dream that was the last bit of his life ebbing away, he thought he heard something. Voices he recognised. The voices of his friends . . .

'Pinch . . . Patch . . .' the murmur began, deep within him. 'Pinch and Patch – friends . . . friends are here . . . They're here . . . they're really here . . . really here . . .' Up and up went the murmur, louder and louder, till it burst from his bloodless lips into the storm-heavy air.

'What's that?' said Euryon, looking down

176

at him, with a face like thunder. 'What's that you say?'

'Friends . . .' said Thomas, very weakly. 'My friends . . . they're here . . . They've come to take me home . . .'

'Well, why didn't you say so before?' growled the giant, and leaning down, he picked Thomas up in his huge fist. 'Didn't know what the heck I was going to do with you, lad, how I could get you back to your own place,' he went on, staring at Thomas with fiery eyes. 'A promise is a promise and I said you'd be safe. And Euryon has never broken a promise.'

Shaking his wild hair, he shouted up at the craft, hovering above him, 'What are you waiting for, fools! Open up!'

'He wants you to open up,' said Patch, desperately, as Hecate still barred the way. 'He's going to give us Thomas!'

'Not on your life,' said Hecate. 'He's the flying huntsman. He never gives up his prey.'

177

'But maybe Thomas isn't his *prey*,' cried Pinch. 'He never planned to get Thomas, did he? It happened because of Astrolir. Please, Signora, open the porthole!'

'Yes, do,' said Ratty, from the controls. 'Do. We only have a little time left before my trick – er my skill – fades away, so hurry up and open that window!'

'Oh, you're all crazy,' said Hecate, crossly, but she opened the porthole, and in the same instant, the flying huntsman threw Thomas up into the air. Patch screamed, and Pinch yelped; but in the next instant, Thomas flew straight in through the opened porthole, and landed on the floor of the craft, where he lay, stunned, winded, and limp, his eyes closed.

'Thomas!' shouted the twins together, rushing to him, trying to hug him, to rub his hands, to bring some colour back into his grey cheeks.

Hecate closed the porthole, and let out her breath very slowly. 'Go! Go like the wind!' she said to Ratty. 'Go, before he changes his mind!'

Around them, the air was darkening, the clouds massing, purple, green, black, taller than mountain ranges, and a howling began that was deeper and wilder than any wind. Outlined against the wild sky, the savage figure of the flying huntsman whirled and rose, up, up, up! Enormous on his enormous winged horse, his pack of ravening hounds by his side, Euryon soared and hovered above them, now plunging towards them, now rising high. The stars in his hair and on his brow and on the brows of his horse and his dogs seemed to dance as the flying huntsman put his horn to his lips and called up the storm. The storm rushed in. Getting bigger and bigger by the instant, it gathered in a huge black wave, racing straight for the city of Seraphimia, where it howled against the walls and shook every building and pounded at the city's defences for many long days, turning daylight into darkness, before the huntsman's fury was

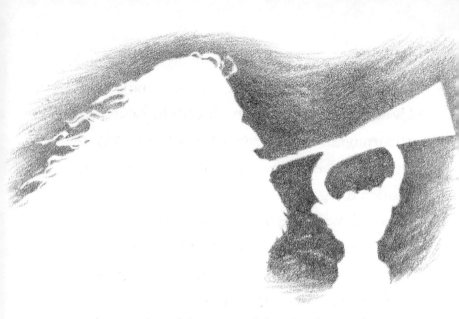

exhausted and he turned his back on the city and rode off to new hunting-grounds, far away.

But the storm did not touch the sun-sailor as it plunged down, out of the dark-cloud-country, away from Seraphimia, and by other paths away from the country of the Ariels and down through a ladder of gentle sun-lit cloud to the welcoming earth.

As it sped on, Pinch and Patch sat anxiously on the floor of the ship and watched Hecate Longnose try all her healing spells on their human friend. They watched as the colour began, very slowly at first, to come back into Thomas's cheeks, and as his breathing began to get stronger. Then he opened his eyes and saw the twins. Shivering, he whispered, 'I . . . I thought I was dead . . .'

'So did we,' breathed Patch, holding tightly to his hand. But Pinch laughed, and said, jauntily, 'Not so easy as that to kill a Rymer, I think! Specially not one like you!'

Thomas tried to smile. 'I'm so glad to see you. I thought you'd gone . . . that you thought that my shadow was the real me . . .'

'Your shadow?' said Hecate. 'Of course! Well, now that Astrolir has gone, that shadow will be back to being what it should be.'

'You have to say that Four Eyes was clever, creep though he was,' said Ratty, earning himself a dark frown from the twins.

'We knew it wasn't you,' said Patch, to Thomas. 'We knew. And so he turned us out into the shadow-land and we had to somehow find our way . . .'

She broke off, because Thomas had closed his eyes again. He was asleep. Hecate said, gently, 'He's still very tired, and very ill, and he's probably going to be unwell for quite a long time. There's an arrow wound in his arm, and his spirit was very close to the end when we found him . . . So you are going to have to be very brave, and very kind, and to help him recover, and not pester him too much with questions and explanations, for a while yet.'

'As if we would!' said Pinch, indignantly, while Patch said, quietly, 'Will he be all right, Signora Longnose?'

'I think so,' said the old witch. 'I think so. You saved him, for you are his true friends, and he will recover. But it will take time, and rest, and good healing.'

'We'll help mother make lots of potions and ointments for him,' cried Patch.

'And stop him from getting bored, if he's got to stay in bed a lot,' said Pinch.

'We'll get him home in a jiffy,' said Ratty. 'Come on, sun-sailor, dear – for that's what you are, really – yes, take that sunbeam path down – and get us down to Owlchurch, and double quick!'

In his dreams, Thomas thought he heard their voices, whispering, and he smiled, deep down inside himself. He was safe, and warm, and he was going home with his friends. His arm still hurt, but it felt a little better. Then, just as he fell into a very deep, healing sleep, he saw, outlined against the darkening screen of his mind, the figure of the flying huntsman, with the bright stars tangled in his hair, rearing on his black horse through the sky, his pack of hounds swirling around his feet. He saw the huntsman raise a huge hand, and heard his rumbling voice call to him across space and time, 'Farewell, Rymer! Farewell!' And then the huntsman threw his head back and played his horn, and instead of the savage storm-cry,

Thomas heard a sweet, silvery, beautiful sound: his mother's song, played on the huntsman's horn, playing on and on, till the sky was filled with it, and the very stars themselves seemed to dance in time to the tune.